D0842183

TIME of DEATH
THE TUNNEL

josh anderson

EPIC
Press

The Tunnel
Time of Death: Book #1

Written by Josh Anderson

Copyright © 2016 by Abdo Consulting Group, Inc.

Published by EPIC Press™
PO Box 398166
Minneapolis, MN 55439

Cover design by Dorothy Toth
Images for cover art obtained from iStockPhoto.com TK
Edited by Ramey Temple

LIBRARY OF CONGRESS CATALOGING-IN-PUBLICATION DATA

Anderson, Josh.
The tunnel / Josh Anderson.
p. cm. — (Time of death ; #1)
Summary: Kyle Cash crashed his friend's Audi into a school bus full of children.
The accident haunts him every day, until he gets the opportunity to travel back in
time. Kyle learns, that time weaving is more complicated—and more
dangerous—than he ever could have imagined.
ISBN 978-1-68076-064-4 (hardcover)
1. Time travel—Fiction. 2. Traffic accidents—Fiction. 3. Life change events—Fic-
tion. 4. Interpersonal relations—Fiction. 5. Conduct of life—Fiction. 6. Guilt—
Fiction. 7. Self-acceptance—Fiction. 8. Young adult fiction. I. Title.
[Fic]—dc23

2015903986

To Corey...
Thank you for being my person.

PROLOGUE

MARCH 13, 2014

K YLE HUNG LIKE A BAT IN THE OVERTURNED Audi. A vampire bat, really, given that he was covered with blood. Next to him, his best friend Joe dangled, unconscious, dripping blood from his mangled face onto the hood of the car. Kyle alternated between screaming for Joe to wake up, and closing his eyes tightly to avoid looking at the upside-down nightmare all around him. *Is there any way for this to turn out okay?* Kyle wondered.

Kyle tried to calm his breathing like that rescue worker guy had told him to. *Deep breaths.* The guy said he'd be right back, but it felt like he'd been gone forever. As Kyle winced from the seatbelt digging deeply into his chest and shivered from the cold morning air coming through his busted windows, he thought to himself, *This can't be what dead feels like.* He was relieved.

Kyle wasn't, however, looking forward to the pounding Joe was going to give him when he woke up and saw how Kyle had wrecked his precious Audi. All because Kyle just couldn't be late for a math test. *Maybe everything could still be okay.* Kyle closed his eyes for a moment.

When he opened them again, Kyle had no idea how long it had been since he'd flipped the car. He heard a loud grinding noise all around him. Now, instead of just seeing the glass-littered pavement of the road, he saw even more legs than before—some standing still, others rushing around.

Then, a face appeared. The same guy, a black dude wearing a 'Rescue Squad' baseball cap. "We're gonna get you out, kid. My name's Bart."

"I'm Kyle. This is Joe. He's bleeding. Please don't leave us again," Kyle whispered, barely opening his mouth to speak. He started shivering again, and closed his eyes once more.

The next time Kyle opened his eyes, he saw even more legs than before. Now, there were red and blue lights flashing, sirens, and backup beeps all around him. He caught bits of intense conversation right outside the window of the overturned Audi. "No survivors." "Divers are just bringing bodies up." "School bus."

When Kyle heard "school bus," he pounded on the seat above him to catch Bart's attention. Kyle's voice was now just a gravely whisper.

"The school bus! It almost hit us," he said.

Suddenly, Bart recoiled. "Oh man, is that . . . ? Is that booze on your breath, kid?" Bart asked, his face all of a sudden disappearing from Kyle's view. "Unbelievable. Un-fucking-believable. This kid's drunk."

Now, Kyle could only see anonymous feet around him again and hear the angry murmuring of the kind man who had been with him until just a second ago. The grinding noise of the Jaws of Life now felt loud enough to swallow him whole.

Kyle closed his eyes once more as he dangled there, hoping there was some way this might turn out okay, but knowing that it probably wouldn't.

CHAPTER 1

KYLE ALMOST DROPPED THE BOTTLE OF TEQUILA into the bathtub when he heard his mother's tires roll over the rocky driveway next to his house. His buddy, Joe, took a long pull on their carefully rolled Dutch Master blunt. The one day they don't wait a few minutes before sparking up, she actually *does* come back home five minutes after she leaves for work. He looked out the tiny bathroom window and saw her getting out of her old, run-down Kia, parked now behind Kyle's equally beat-up '96 Nissan Sentra. The car was one of the only things his father left behind when he bolted.

"Shit, it's my mom," Kyle said. "What are we

gonna do? The second I open this door, the whole upstairs is gonna reek."

Joe shrugged his shoulders and grabbed the tequila—lifted from Joe's dad's endless stash. "It's your house, man. I don't know." Joe swigged another shot, and then hit the blunt again, craning his neck toward the window, then pursing his lips. He slowly exhaled a huge plume of marijuana smoke through the screen.

"I wouldn't worry so much, man," Joe said a few seconds later. "Anyone who would choose this fuckin' wallpaper had to be a pothead at some point." Kyle was so used to seeing the pattern at this point that it didn't feel weird anymore, but green elephants walking on a tightrope, balancing huge, silver platters with their trunks was pretty weird.

"Put it out, dude," Kyle said. "And disappear the bottle."

Joe took one more hit, holding the smoke inside for as long as he could before exhaling. His chubby face looked even huger as he puffed out his smoke-filled cheeks. This time, Joe completely forgot to aim for the window. Then, he opened his mouth and used his tongue to extinguish the fiery cherry at the end of the blunt. He tucked the tequila bottle into the deep pocket of his XXL North Face jacket.

I'm fucked, Kyle thought to himself. His mom had never caught him smoking pot before. Not red-handed, at least. She was definitely one of those moms who was okay with looking the other way now and then, as long as she didn't feel like Kyle was taking advantage—and as long as his grades were good, which had never been a problem. So much of high school grading was based on memorization, and there was no one in the county with a better memory than his. But 'hotboxing' Stella Cash's upstairs bathroom—the one she showered in every morning—was definitely not a betrayal that the woman who'd raised him by herself would be willing to ignore. He had a big weekend planned too. *There has to be a way to make this turn out okay.*

He heard the front door open, and the screen door slam shut behind his mother. For a moment, Kyle debated whether they should quickly exit the bathroom, go downstairs, and hope his mother didn't notice that they reeked of weed. Or, should they just wait it out quietly and pray she left before she realized that they hadn't left for school yet.

The lock on the upstairs bathroom was uselessly placed on the outside of the door, so if she tried to come in, they were screwed. Quite the scene she'd be walking into: her son and his best friend, winter coats and backpacks on, their Timberlands neatly lined up on her bathroom floor, standing in her empty bathtub for a little wake-and-bake before school.

Kyle grabbed a bottle of mouthwash from under the sink. He took a swig, and handed the bottle over to Joe. Kyle swished it around his mouth fast, and then spit it toward the shower drain. He closed his eyes and pictured the downstairs of the house, wondering if he'd left anything down there that would signal to his mother that he was still home. There were four dishes in the sink. The small side table where his mother kept her wallet was empty.

Joe gargled for a second, looked around aimlessly, and then swallowed. "Ahh . . . " he said, as if it were another shot of the tequila. "Prolly should've smoked outside, huh?"

This wasn't their normal move—drinking and getting high before school in Ms. Cash's upstairs bathroom. Usually, they played video games in Kyle's basement until she left, and then smoked a little in the backyard, or in one of their cars.

Today was even bleaker and colder than usual for a winter day in Flemming. Plus, the heat in Kyle's car wasn't working, which was particularly bad timing due to the super-chilly stretch, even by upstate New York standards. The normally picturesque landscape was littered by dirt-speckled, hilly remnants of frozen snow on the sides of every road which hadn't gotten a chance to melt since the two-foot snowstorm last week. Black ice made the late nights and early mornings treacherous on the roads. During this cold streak, the only time most days that Kyle went outside voluntarily was when he and Joe, and some of their other friends, would sneak away into the huge field behind Silverman High School for a midday smoke break.

"Shhh . . . " Kyle said to Joe, listening for his mother's footsteps. "If we get caught, there's no way she's letting me go to Randall's Island this weekend." He heard her walking around downstairs. If she never came up, they'd be fine. Even if she did, they had toweled the door. Kyle used his hands to fan the air in the room toward the window, as if he could just push out the unmistakable, sticky smell of cheap weed. He didn't want to miss the *Winter Riot* music festival this weekend, and since his mom had been on the fence about letting him go anyway, there was no doubt what his punishment would be if she caught them this morning.

He had trouble tracking where his mother was in the house. First, the footsteps sounded close by, and then distant, and then close once again. He was clearly fucked up—definitely high, and a little drunk too. Then, the footsteps suddenly stopped. *Maybe*, Kyle thought, *this can still turn out okay.*

"Kyle, are you here . . . ?" his mom called out. It sounded like she was right at the bottom of the stairs. *Decision time.*

"Did you drive here or walk?" Kyle whispered to Joe.

"Walked."

"I told her you might be driving me today," Kyle whispered. "She might think my car's here because you picked me up. Let's just stay quiet." Kyle caught a glimpse of himself in the mirror and noticed his bloodshot eyes. He didn't like mirrors when he was high. He'd been lucky enough for girls to find him good looking, but whenever he caught a glimpse of his spiky brown hair and angular cheekbones when he'd been smoking pot, he felt like his hard features made him look monstrous.

Joe held the extinguished blunt in front of his face. "You mind if I keep this, or you want it?" Even though Kyle had the better weed hookup, Joe was the bigger pothead. If they weren't best friends, Kyle might've made a bigger deal out of paying for ninety percent of the weed they smoked, especially since Joe's family gave him forty bucks a week for allowance and Kyle gave his whole paycheck from the dry cleaner to his mom to help with bills.

Kyle pushed Joe's hand away and moved his head as close as he could get it to the door without falling out of the shower.

"Is someone there?" Ms. Cash yelled. "Hello?"

Kyle thought he heard footsteps right outside the door and stepped over the edge of the tub to listen. *We still may be okay*, he thought to himself. *Maybe she's looking for something in her bedroom.* He grabbed a can of Lysol off the top of a bathroom cabinet and pressed the dispenser button gently, as if a light press could make it spray more quietly.

Joe clumsily climbed out of the bathtub and was about to pick up one of his boots when Kyle grabbed his hand. "Wait," he said.

Kyle heard the footsteps get faster and louder. He smiled. Then, the unmistakable screech of the screen door opening downstairs and the front door slamming shut. He and Joe did their patented 'spooky hands' high five, perfect for a moment just like this.

"I have no idea what she forgot," Kyle said. "Everything she normally takes was gone when we came up."

"You're a freak," Joe answered.

"Eidetic people have feelings too," Kyle said with a laugh, referring to his photographic, or 'eidetic,' memory. It wasn't like a superpower—Kyle didn't *try* to use it, but he could recall nearly any image in perfect detail, even if he'd only seen it for a very short time.

Kyle climbed back into the tub, and pressed his face against the window screen. He saw his mom holding her lunch cooler and standing next to her car with her hands on her hips, looking around. After a few seconds, she walked toward the back of the driveway and peeked into the backyard as if she had heard something. Then, she walked back to her car, shaking her head. "Hello?" he heard her call out. He wished he wasn't so high, so he could go out and see what was going on. His mom looked a little freaked out, and Kyle felt bad. Perhaps she'd heard them, or sensed that someone else was around.

After checking the backyard, his mom got back in her car and headed off.

Kyle sprayed enough Lysol to disinfect a small city before they hurried out of the bathroom, leaving the door and window open. He had enough faith in his memory to know that he'd remember to close the window later when he got home.

Kyle checked the clock hanging at the top of

the stairs—twenty minutes until his logic quiz in first period math. He hadn't expected math to be his easiest class of second semester, junior year, but Kyle had been doing logic puzzles for fun since he was a little kid. Being a little high and drunk would make it more fun for him. He had nothing to worry about as long as he could get himself to first period in time. "We've got to hustle, dude," he said, bouncing downstairs.

Kyle turned around to see Joe taking his time behind him. Joe Stropoli wasn't the world's best hustler. In fact, Joe didn't really march to anyone's beat but his own. Kyle wanted to have fun, be a little irresponsible, and then prove he could still get things done when he needed to. Joe, on the other hand, just didn't give a shit.

Kyle ran to the basement to grab his phone. He picked up Joe's too, and then bolted up the basement stairs two at a time. He handed Joe his phone, opened the front door, and stood there waiting. "Joe, I have a fuckin' quiz. C'mon, man!"

Joe started messing with his phone and almost walked into a wall. "This game is sick when you're high," he said, pushing past Kyle and out the door. Kyle noticed a couple of leaves on the stairs, courtesy of Joe's shoes, and picked them up with his hands.

Kyle saw that his car's front tire on the driver's side was flat. "Shit," he said. "Of course, this morning." He walked around to the other side, and the front passenger tire was completely slack around the wheel too. Definitely not drivable. *Two flats?* he thought. *Unusual.* Not that Kyle would know much about 'usual' having only had his license for a couple of months.

"We've gotta take your car," Kyle said.

"No way," Joe answered. "I'm too fucked up to drive today. The morning cocktails did me in." Joe let out that big laugh of his which was usually directed at something he'd said himself.

"C'mon, man," Kyle asked again.

Joe started walking out of the driveway, toward

his house. "Who cares? You think math class really matters? Let's go chill at my house, play some Madden, and then I'll drive us to school later. Your nerdy ass will make it to half your classes today, at least."

They lived about ten minutes from Silverman High, which was exactly how long Kyle had until his math teacher, Mr. Meltzner, locked the classroom door to keep out any latecomers.

"Please, Joe," Kyle said. "You know I care about my grades, bro."

"We're both fucked up. Better safe than sorry," Joe said. "Especially today, man, with all the black ice out there." But, Kyle had seen Joe drive high plenty. If they were going to a party, or to get more weed, or just cruising around, Joe would never have said the first thing about staying off the road. But, if it meant they could just chill out and eat a second breakfast, Joe was happy to conveniently argue for safety first.

Sometimes Kyle wished he could be as indifferent

as Joe about school, and really, about everything that mattered. Kyle didn't have that luxury, though. His mom wasn't going to be able to pay for college if he didn't get a scholarship.

"The adrenaline rush from my mom coming home totally sobered me up," Kyle said. "Let me drive us in your car." Kyle knew he was wasting his breath. He'd have to start talking Joe's language.

Joe headed toward the front door of his house, which was twice the size of Kyle's. "You comin' inside?"

"No. I'm walkin' to school," Kyle said.

Joe looked genuinely surprised. "Seriously? You're gonna freeze your nuts off."

"Yeah," Kyle said. "I better take the rest of that blunt to keep me warm on the walk." He knew Joe didn't have any weed at home.

"You're a dick," Joe said.

"Yeah, but I'm a dick who's gonna smoke the rest of that blunt without you," Kyle said. "Come on, man, let's just go to school."

Joe took off his backpack and grabbed his keys from inside. He tossed them to Kyle, and walked over to the passenger side of his Audi.

"You better drive real careful," Joe said, tossing a balled up McDonald's bag from the passenger seat onto the floor. "Remember, you're driving a finely tuned piece of European engineering. This isn't your shitty fuckin' Nissan."

Before Kyle could start the car, Joe sparked the blunt again using his most prized possession, a Zippo lighter with a pot leaf design in the colors of the Jamaican flag. He had only let Kyle drive his Audi once before.

Of all the many ways their lives were different because Joe's family had money and Kyle's mom did not, Kyle had never noticed it more than when he drove Joe's car. His eighteen-year-old Sentra would buck and resist at every opportunity as he pushed it closer and closer to a quarter of a million miles.

Joe's brand new Audi felt like it was bred from

a champion racehorse and a rocket ship, ready to serve his every whim behind the wheel. It was damn fun to drive, and if Kyle was ever going to cut the ten-minute drive to school in half, he was in the right car to do it.

CHAPTER 2

MARCH 13, 2014

moments later

As the 'Cheese Bus' hit another pothole, Scarlett looked around at each of the eighth graders and one-by-one thought to herself: "Moron," "Bully," "Racist," "Psycho," "Wimp." Scarlett hoped every day that it wasn't her turn to be singled out by the assholes in the back, especially stupid Lisa Cartigliani.

Scarlett faced backward, sitting on her knees, watching the cruel stupidity of the day unfold around her. This time, Lisa and her cousin Tiffany were using a ruler to measure poor Marlon's lips while he slept. They were rank-and-file members of the popular clique at school, but the unopposed Queens of Bus #17.

"Holy shit!" Lisa called out, laughing. "One and seven eighths wide, and two inches tall. His lips are, like, twice as plump as mine!"

Etan Rachnowitz laughed louder than anyone else. He must've liked Lisa, Scarlett thought, because he laughed at every dumb thing she said. "Even you gotta admit that's crazy, Snodgrass!"

Tom Snodgrass looked more like a menacing 20-year-old than a middle-schooler. Broad-shouldered and tall, he had decisively opted out of the Cheese Bus's social strata in favor of quietly reading *Star Trek* novels. Nobody bothered him.

When Tom refused to look up and give Etan the moment of validation he craved, Etan looked at Scarlett and pushed out his lips, imitating the way Marlon looked as he slept. Afraid her moment would come sooner if she didn't, Scarlett smiled.

Etan took a piece of gum out of his mouth and rolled it into a ball. "Check it out," he said.

He held the chewed gum above Marlon's lips and looked at Lisa for approval.

"No way!" Lisa said, with a giggle.

"No, dude," Tom called out, barely looking up from his book. Then, louder: "Do not do it."

Poor Marlon slept, unaware of any of this, his lips pursed into a perfect little pocket just right for an asshole like Etan to ditch his gum there.

Etan gave one last look at Tom, who kept reading, but was clearly monitoring the situation. Everyone else on the bus was glued to the proceedings by the time Etan gently placed the chewed-up gum right onto Marlon's lips.

"We gotta wake him up," Lisa said cheerfully, climbing over the seats in front of her. She put both hands up to Marlon's face and started alternating slaps. Gently at first, but then harder as he barely stirred. She pushed the gum further into his lips, so it was mostly inside his mouth.

Disgusting, Scarlett thought.

Lisa was growing impatient. Finally, she reared

back her hand and laid a full-on skin-stinger to his cheek.

She backed away as Marlon's eyes opened. He chewed the gum for a second, then pushed it out of his mouth with his tongue. He looked confused, as everyone just stared and laughed.

Marlon looked down at the gum on the floor.

"Your lips looked lonely, bro," Etan said. "My gum fit there perfectly." Marlon looked up at Etan, and Scarlett could see the tears well up in his eyes, and then quickly overflow. He buried his head in his lap.

"You're crying, bro?" Etan said. "It was just a joke."

While everyone watched Marlon break down, Scarlett noticed out of the corner of her eye that Tom had gotten out of his seat and was standing right behind Etan now. Tom quickly threw his arm around Etan's neck and put him in a chokehold from behind. Etan's stunned face quickly gave way to a panicked look. He grabbed at Tom's adult-sized arm and tried to pull it off of him.

"You don't fucking listen," Tom said quietly in the direction of Etan's ear, pulling his own wrist with his free hand to tighten up the pressure of the chokehold. Within a few seconds, Etan's face turned bright red as he struggled to get Tom off of him. Scarlett wondered how long he could handle being choked without getting seriously hurt.

She turned to look at Bruno, the driver, and noticed him watching the boys through his rear-view mirror. He generally let the kids do whatever they wanted, but she was scared that this could get out of control. She was relieved to feel the bus pull onto gravel and slow down.

Bruno stopped the bus, stood up, and walked toward them. "Are you sick in the head?" he screamed at Tom in his heavy accent. "Put him down!"

By now, Etan's face was a shade beyond the worst sunburn Scarlett could imagine. He lifted his legs in the air, trying to kick himself out as Tom stoically held the chokehold in place, his face completely void of emotion.

"Get the hell off of him!" Bruno screamed, grabbing Tom's forearm now. Tom held on for a couple more seconds before letting go. Etan crumbled to the ground and quickly pulled himself up to Tom's seat as he gasped for air.

"Sit down," Bruno said to Tom. Then, he bent down to Etan. "You alright, kid?"

Etan didn't even acknowledge Bruno. Instead, he stood up and pushed past the crowd to take his usual seat in the back, across from Lisa and Tiffany's row. Now, it was Etan who looked close to tears.

"Listen, all of you," Bruno said. "Let's just get to school without any more, uh . . . stupidity, okay? No more fighting." His Italian accent made it sound more authoritative, which was good, because Tom's blank stare made it look like he wanted to finish what he started.

What a bunch of assholes, Scarlett thought to herself, ashamed she didn't have the courage to say it out loud.

CHAPTER 3

KYLE SLOWED UP JUST A TINY BIT AS HE PASSED by his old middle school. He knew the cops could be real hard asses about speeding in school zones. He wished he had five extra minutes to spare. Since he didn't, he pushed the Audi up to sixty on Avanti Drive.

"We get pulled over, you're paying," Joe said.

"We're not getting pulled over," Kyle answered. Slush kicked up from under the tires as he accelerated through the middle stretch of each block, only to come to one stop sign after another. When he saw the time, he felt panicky. It was 8:53—he had seven minutes until he had to be in his seat in class.

They usually saved drinking for weekends. And even though Kyle didn't feel that much more fucked up than most mornings, he hoped being drunk, too, wouldn't impact his math test—assuming he made it to school in time.

He turned onto Canarsie Road and felt the tires skid just a little on the slick ground. He had no choice but to floor it. He saw someone three blocks ahead crossing the street with a dog.

"You think it's messed up that I don't care if we get to school for first period?" Joe asked. "I think my priorities may be all wrong, man. That's what my dad says."

Kyle looked at his friend. "This is what you always do, dude," Kyle said, trying to half-focus on Joe's existential crisis. "We smoke, and then for a little while you're happy. And then you get all paranoid and self . . . self-something. Take a deep breath. You're fine." When Kyle glanced back at the road ahead, the person with the dog was still in the middle of the road. It looked like they were crossing in slow motion.

"No, Kyle. *You're* fine. Somehow, it always works out for you. You can party, and hang, and do whatever, and you still get A's and keep your mom off your ass. Sometimes I wish I was the one without a dad."

Kyle had no patience for Joe's spoiled self-pity. He tried to catch his eye with a look. Sometimes that was the best way to remind his friend that he was talking crazy. When he turned to glance back at the road, the person with the dog was still in the middle of the street, but all of a sudden they were only twenty feet away. Kyle switched lanes without looking over his shoulder and pressed on the accelerator. It wasn't quite a full swerve, but it was enough to get his heart racing. As he passed her, the woman with the dog looked at him and just shook her head in that disapproving old lady kind of way.

"What the fuck, bro?" Joe asked.

"Sorry," Kyle said with a relieved laugh. "You're just saying such dumb shit, I got distracted." Kyle didn't talk very often about the fact that he had no memory of ever meeting his own father, but Joe being so oblivious still pissed him off.

Kyle slowed down, realizing he was going close to seventy now on residential streets. Now, he just had to drive up and down the hill on Nairn Boulevard and over Banditt Drawbridge and they'd be cruising into the Silverman High parking lot. He estimated that this was about three minutes away if he pushed it, which he had to, because it was 8:56.

Kyle loved that he barely had to press the Audi's gas for it to climb the large hill. "This is so much better because I'm high," he said to Joe. "I feel like I'm a pilot right now. That weed actually wasn't so bad."

"Don't forget the tequila, dude," Joe answered. "That shit is like seventy dollars a bottle. *Te gusta*, eh?"

They came to the top of Nairn Boulevard, the highest point in Flemming, New York. Normally, they might stop for a few extra seconds up here, taking in the view of the Hudson, but not today.

The school itself was obscured by oak trees, but Kyle could see the Silverman High baseball diamond in the distance as he came down the hill. Even his Sentra could get going a little too fast on the way down Nairn, but today Kyle put his faith in Joe's Audi handling the slick pavement. He needed a miracle to make it to class in time. It was 8:58, and he still had to cross the drawbridge and park.

He sped down the end of the hill and onto Banditt Drawbridge, tapping the brake as he felt the car jerk a bit when it rolled onto the metal grating. A small school bus—probably on its way to the middle school—was at the other end of the drawbridge about a hundred yards ahead.

He saw the bus up ahead swerve into his lane. As it continued rolling toward them, Kyle saw it wobble slightly over the yellow line a second time, then correct itself. He gripped the wheel tighter as he neared the bus. There was an older man behind the wheel. The bus's number was 17—Kyle's lucky number. *A good omen*, he thought, for his odds of making it to his math quiz.

He looked down at the clock again: 8:59. Then he pressed his foot against the gas pedal, and spoke quickly, "Joe, listen, when we get to school, I'm driving up to the main entrance and jumping out. Park it yourself."

Joe scrunched up his face and looked offended. "Why? So *I* can be late for first period?"

"You don't even care, man! You were ready to skip the whole day," Kyle shouted, giving Joe a look.

Joe reached over and grabbed Kyle's sleeve to get his attention, clearly pissed off. "Just because you get straight A's and I don't, doesn't mean that you getting to first period is more important than me getting to first period. You are so fuckin' selfish, Kyle!"

Kyle yanked his arm away. "I'm selfish? Joe, you don't even—"

Joe cut Kyle off, "Squirrel!"

Kyle barely caught a glimpse of the fluffy tail before he swerved sharply left, over the double yellow line.

When the car first went airborne, Kyle thought it was just a small bump from running over the squirrel. He even got an 'ooh' out of his mouth before the roof of the car slammed into the east guardrail of the drawbridge. The Audi flung the other way now, flipping over again as it bounced from one side of the drawbridge to the other. The car went side-over-side three times in what felt like only a second or two before skidding to a stop, with its tires in the air and its roof against the ground.

Kyle hung upside down, still strapped in. He looked around, trying to figure out where he was, what side of the bridge, the squirrel, Joe, the bus? He checked the clock and felt a pang of disappointment to see the digital numbers change to 9:01—officially late for his quiz. Kyle touched his body and face. There was blood splattered everywhere, and he felt sharp pieces of glass all over him. He couldn't be sure, but he *seemed* okay. He felt a great sense of relief until he looked over at Joe. When he saw his best friend, Kyle let out an audible gag.

Less than a mile away, Paul Meltzner stood up to lock his classroom door and hand out his logic quiz to the class. *Kyle Cash is late again*, he thought to himself. *Smart kid, but he needs to get off the Mary Jane.*

CHAPTER 4

JANUARY 31, 2016

two years later

KYLE HELD OCHOA'S LONG, CURLY HAIR BACK behind his head as his huge cellmate puked over the toilet.

"I never shoulda drank that stuff, bro," Ochoa said, practically in tears. "I feel like I'm gonna die."

Kyle helped guide his head toward the toilet again. The last thing he wanted was for their cell to smell like puke for the next month. Another orangey spew shot from Ochoa's mouth toward the water. Kyle winced as a drop from the toilet splashed out onto his arm. He quickly wiped it off with toilet paper and wiped off the seat as well.

"Just get it out, Och." He was eager for this to

be over. Ochoa had been bragging about making his own prison wine, or *pruno*, for months. He took apples from the Stevenson Youth Correctional Facility mess hall and fermented them in plastic bags under his mattress. Kyle had a feeling he wasn't doing it right the first time he saw him squeezing a few drops of juice out of a moldy apple, but Trevor Ochoa wasn't one of those people you could convince when he got his mind onto something. So now, Kyle played nursemaid to the grumpy giant.

Kyle had been terrified when, right after receiving his eight-year manslaughter sentence, he arrived by bus at Stevenson Youth Correctional in New York City and found himself sharing a cell with a six-foot-four Puerto Rican with neck tats and arms thicker than Kyle's legs. It took a few weeks, but Kyle realized that Ochoa was a decent person—like him, a guy who had made a mistake.

Kyle was in the middle of a dream when Ochoa's retching woke him up this morning. It wasn't the crash dream—the one where he manages to avoid hitting the bus altogether. It was one about Billy and Frankie Costello, or maybe it was Patty Marshall. All of the kids Kyle had killed on Bus #17 had shown up in his dreams more times than he could count. The kids he knew more about, from the newspaper coverage of the crash and from stalking their dormant Facebook pages, tended to show up in his dreams most often. The more details he knew, the easier it was to torture himself and imagine them as the living, breathing people they'd all been before the crash.

Ochoa spewed violently once more, then took a deep breath. "That's a little better," Ochoa said, wiping the corners of his mouth with the inside of his khaki, state-issued shirt.

"Wash your hands real good, Och . . . Your grandma comin' today?" Kyle asked. "She hasn't seen you with a hangover since you got sent up, huh?"

Ochoa stood up. He stretched his arms and shoulders above his head and then got down into pushup position. "Think you could beat me today?" he asked with a glint in his eye.

"Stop showing off, Och," Kyle answered. Kyle could do fifty, on a good day. Ochoa wasn't only built like a strong safety, but he would knock out two hundred and fifty push-ups at least twice a day. It was his way of getting out some of that extra energy one tends to have when cooped up in a ninety-six-square-foot cell for eighteen hours a day.

"Grandma's got something with my little brother today," Ochoa said, starting his pushups. "Math Olympics or somethin' . . . One . . . Two . . . Three . . . Four . . . "

Kyle laid down, hoping he might be able to fall asleep again. There were no classes on Saturdays, and no rec time until later in the afternoon. Usually, Kyle tried to sleep through morning visiting hours. He looked at the one picture hanging above his bunk—a shot of him and his mom playing on the beach from a vacation they'd taken to the Jersey shore when he was seven. Looking at it calmed him, and reminded him there was more to the world than what went on inside of Stevenson Youth Correctional.

"Anyone coming to see your bitch-ass today?" Ochoa asked, barely winded as he continued his push-ups.

Before he could answer, Kyle heard a rapping on the door, and then the lock turning over. Officer Radbourn stepped inside and both boys stood up—a regulation of the detention center.

"Seventeen years I been working here, since the day the place opened," Radbourn said. "And still, I can't get used to how scared you little pricks look whenever a guard comes in for inspection. Almost makes me feel bad."

Radbourn was kind of an asshole, but he was the only guard at Stevenson Correctional who didn't make a habit of robbing the inmates of their dignity or their possessions.

"Trevor, *donde esta abuela y hermano* this week?" Radbourn asked. "They finally give up on your sorry ass?" He laughed loudly while Och just stared at him.

"She's with my brother," Ochoa said. "She ain't comin'."

"Cash Man, your father comes to visit all the way from . . . " Radbourn stared down at the clipboard in his hand, "all the way from Jacksonville and you don't even comb your hair? C'mon kid."

Kyle's dad was so far out of the picture that the image of him in Kyle's head was of a guy in his early twenties holding Kyle as an infant—the one photograph his mother had kept of his father. *He isn't here,* Kyle thought. *There'd be no reason.* "Eat me, Rad."

"I'm serious, asshole. Get up and comb your hair," Radbourn said. "Sillow Cash of 1363 Seaview Avenue, Jacksonville, Florida. Says on my sheet that he's your father. He's in the visiting area now. What? You didn't know he was coming?"

What the hell is my father doing here? Kyle wondered to himself. He'd thought a million times about what he'd say to his dad if he ever saw him again, but his mind was blank now. He'd found a phone number for his father last year and left a voicemail inviting him to be at Kyle's mother's funeral, but he never showed.

Kyle walked toward the door of his cell in a daze. "Alright," he said, running a comb through his hair. "Let's go."

Radbourn put his hand on Kyle's shoulder. "You know I'm just fucking with you . . . You alright? I didn't even know your old man was around. Thought he was a deadbeat like—"

"—He is, and I don't have anything to say to him," Kyle answered. "This'll be quick."

Kyle could feel himself shutting down mentally, something he had done each day during his trial. It was the only way to get through a process where every single person around you has come to work for the day with the express purpose of deciding how much you should be punished for the horrible thing you did. And, all of them—even the ones working for you—look nauseated to be in your presence. Kyle trained himself, over those two months, to almost come out of his body on his days in court. He observed the process as if it were happening to a stranger. The biggest torture he faced was having the realization over and over that there was nothing he could do to make things *okay* again for the kids from Bus #17, or for their families—nothing at all.

Stevenson Correctional used its auditorium as its visitor's center, too. The room had good natural acoustics, so the buzz of fifty different conversations going on at once was jarring at first, especially coming from a calm Saturday morning in Dormitory H with most of the other inmates sleeping.

Radbourn pointed out his father, sitting and waiting for Kyle, looking antsy in his small wooden chair. Sillow dabbed at his forehead with a paper towel. The age difference aside, Kyle's memory of the way Sillow looked from the picture was pretty dead-on with the man in front of him. Kyle stood there for a little while, gathering himself before walking over.

Kyle usually blamed only himself for crashing into the bus on the drawbridge and killing twelve kids and their driver. He'd been the one to get high and drunk. He'd been speeding. He'd let Joe distract him from the road.

Every night, he read their names on the piece of notebook paper taped to his wall—his personal memorial to them. He did everything he could to keep the kids alive, at least in his memory. It was the least he could do, since the bus crash was something he could never make *okay*, no matter what he did.

Every once in a while, though, when Kyle felt like spreading the blame around a little bit, he turned his thoughts to his father. *What,* Kyle wondered, *would life have been like if I'd had a father around?*

Sillow stood up when he saw Kyle, and

straightened his wrinkly button-down. Kyle looked past him at first, not wanting to give him the satisfaction that he had recognized him so easily.

"Hey," Sillow said, as Kyle closed in on him.

"Hey."

Sillow extended his hand to Kyle, but Kyle just let it hang there. "You wanna sit?" Sillow asked, stepping out of the row of theater-style seats to let Kyle in.

"You wanna tell me why you're here?" Kyle asked.

Sillow looked deep into his eyes. "You don't remember, do you? Neither of us were sure what you'd remember."

"Uh . . . No, I *don't* remember you, Dad," Kyle said, already annoyed at him. "I remember one picture . . . I remember my mother seeming broken until the day she died because you left us for your new family . . . What are you doing here?"

"Wait, Kyle . . . That's not what I—" Sillow started.

"Oh? That's not what you came to talk about?" Kyle asked. "Fuck you."

"Dammit. I should've waited another day," Sillow said. "I just wanted to make sure I caught you before—"

Kyle stood up. *What was he talking about—waiting another day?* he thought to himself. "Don't come here again."

"Just sit down, please," Sillow said, dabbing his head again with a paper. "I need to tell you some things."

What could he have to say that I would care about? Kyle wondered. He wanted to deny this time to his father. For once, in their relationship, Kyle got to call the shots. But, curiosity got the better of Kyle for the moment and he sat down on the arm of one of the auditorium chairs.

"This doesn't need to be confrontational between us," Sillow said. "I know I've done a lot that was wrong. But I'm tryin' to make it better. I swear I am . . ."

Before Kyle could say anything, a tall woman with her chestnut hair tied into a long braid, moved loudly down the aisle toward them. She clutched her purse as her heels clicked against the floor. She looked like she was in a rush. "Excuse me," she said.

Sillow stood up and the woman brushed past him in the narrow aisle, her bag practically smacking him as she passed. Kyle stood up from the armrest to let her pass too.

"Sorry. Excuse me," she said again.

After she passed, Kyle noticed something on the ground. He bent down to pick it up and saw it was a wallet sized photo of Sillow with a woman about his age, and two little girls. The picture looked like it was taken a while ago by a professional, in a park somewhere. They looked happy, happier than Kyle could remember ever seeing his mom, with a small number of exceptions.

"Nice family," Kyle said, handing the picture to Sillow. "Do they know about me? Or Mom?"

Sillow wrinkled his forehead as he looked at the picture. "This picture isn't—"

"—Yeah, I thought so," Kyle said. "If you didn't care enough to take some responsibility for almost eighteen years, why start now? You should get back to your real family, Sillow."

"You don't understand," Sillow said.

"I have to admit," Kyle said. "I used to be a little jealous when Mom told me about your perfect little set up in Florida. But, now? I just pity them, because they're stuck with you." Kyle's voice cracked getting out those last words. It felt good to unload on his father. He turned and started to walk away. *Don't look back*, he said to himself. *Do not look back.*

"I need to tell you something," Sillow called out after him. "I failed! The whole thing . . . It didn't work!"

Kyle walked to one of the guards, a tall twenty-something guy named Andrews. "I'm good," he said to Andrews.

"Transport," Andrews said grumpily into his walkie-talkie. "Inmate Cash to Dorm H."

Kyle felt someone behind him and turned to find Sillow there. His father looked frazzled now, trying to get words out faster than his mouth could move. "You've got to listen to me . . . Just listen . . . You can't change anything . . . I don't think it's even possible. Just tell them 'no.' I tried . . . I did what you told me . . . "

Sillow put his hand on Kyle's shoulder, but Andrews stepped in between them. "No touching," he growled.

"Please," Sillow screamed as Andrews led Kyle out of the auditorium.

Kyle turned and looked at Sillow once more. *Did what you told me? What the hell was he talking about?* he wondered. Then he thought about the picture of Sillow's happy family. *Who cares?* He thought, as anger washed over him and he walked back to his cell.

CHAPTER 5

SATURDAY AFTERNOONS WERE LEISURE TIME. FOR some inmates at Stevenson Correctional, that meant hoops in the yard, or a walk around the grounds of the prison for some fresh air. For Kyle, it meant Internet research on the kids he'd killed in the bus accident on March 13, almost two years earlier. It was not an activity that would qualify as "leisure" to most people. But, he was very protective of this time, which he'd sworn to his victims. He'd studied them until there was literally nothing more to learn.

Kyle would take up residence in the prison's computer lab from lunchtime until right before dinner on Saturdays without fail. A guy who wasn't gang-affiliated could wind up getting beat up, or worse, for squatting on one of the computers like Kyle did. But Ochoa never failed to quickly end any threats that came Kyle's way.

No one bothered getting to know people after they died, and Kyle felt that *that* was at least part of the finality of what made someone Dead with a capital 'D.' Seeing a family member's Facebook recollection, or finding an old school picture he'd never seen, made the kids who died on Bus #17 just the tiniest bit alive to him for a moment. He collected information about the kids as if it would eventually add up to a complete set, like baseball cards.

Ridiculous as it may have seemed to anyone else, he never wavered from his Saturday afternoon tradition of Internet stalking the dead kids of Bus #17. Kyle's photographic memory allowed him to collect these facts and images in his mind forever—making for more detailed and comprehensive ways to torture himself.

His father's visit had caused him the inconvenience of being stuck today with the slowest of the three 1990s-era PCs. It also had a sticky keyboard from someone's juice or soda spilling on it.

Just as Kyle began to settle into Lisa Carigliani's stagnant Facebook page, the door to the lab opened and a mountainous guard, Officer Gee, stared his way. "You already had a visitor today, didn't you Cash?"

Kyle nodded.

"You're real popular," Gee said. "Let's go."

Kyle stood up from the computer, but didn't move toward the door. "If it's my father again—"

"It's a lady," Gee said. "Let's go! Fuckin' hustle. Visitors are a privilege. You want it taken away from you?"

Kyle hadn't had a visitor since before his mom's suicide last year. Now, two in one day. *Very strange,* he thought. He walked behind Gee down the same corridor as earlier. When they entered the auditorium, Gee pointed him to the chestnut haired woman with the braid. It was the same woman who had been sitting right near Kyle and his dad earlier.

Kyle walked up, skeptical that there wasn't some mistake. When he gave her another look, the woman looked slightly familiar to him, but he couldn't place her. "Do we know each other?" he asked.

"We do. We've never met, but we do. I'm Myrna Rachnowitz," she said, extending her hand frostily.

Immediately, Kyle knew. He'd been to her Facebook page. "Etan's sister, right?" If he hadn't done detailed research on their family he might've assumed she was Etan's mother. He shook her clammy hand.

In his folder of articles about the crash, he had a clipping from a *Flemming Weekly Press* article with the text of the eulogy Myrna gave at the school's memorial service. Kyle remembered it by heart. The ending was beautiful:

They haven't passed away; they've ascended.
They haven't died; they've been born into another world.
They may have been taken from us, but that they were given to us in the first place is a miracle.

"Hi," he said.

When he was first sentenced, Kyle expected that he'd get visits from time to time from angry family members of "The Children of Bus #17," as the national media called them. But, it hadn't happened that way, the long trial perhaps giving everyone the closure they needed.

"I want you to know, I don't hate you," Myrna said. "My little brother had a devilish streak too. I had the daddy who was a deadbeat, and I became an overachieving corporate lawyer. When my mom remarried, she picked the dearest, most responsible man you could imagine. They had my brother in their forties and he was a handful and a half for them." Based on Kyle's research, Etan had been a bully, plain and simple. But, even bullies had people who loved them. And, of course, no one in middle school was doomed to be any one thing forever.

Myrna shifted in her seat. She was poised and confident, but clearly choosing her words carefully. Kyle wondered why she was there.

"I'm sure Etan would've gotten into his share of trouble too," she said. "Most boys your age make mistakes . . . They're just usually lucky enough not to have a bus and a bridge, and twelve kids, on the other end of their bad decisions."

"Listen," Kyle said with a bit of impatience in his voice, "not a day goes by that I don't . . . "

"No," Myrna said, "that's not why I'm here. You don't have to . . . I mean, I'm not here to . . . " she cleared her throat and leaned in closer to Kyle.

"We have an opportunity," she said. "We're going to get you out of here."

"*Out* of here?" Kyle asked, looking around nervously now. "I don't understand."

Myrna smiled politely at him. "Out of prison."

"Ms. Rachno—" Kyle started.

She put her hand up to stop him. "Unfortunately, it's not as simple as opening the door to your cell and walking out. See, you made your bed in the here and now. I can't change the fact that you were sentenced to eight years any more than you can." She paused. "But, what if I told you it was possible to go back?"

"Go back? Go back where?" Kyle asked.

"Not where," Myrna answered, lowering her voice again. "*When* . . . What if I said I could give you the chance to go back in time and change the events leading up to the bus crash so that it never happens in the first place?"

Kyle searched for words. She appeared so put together at first that he was surprised to hear her sound so crazy. "I am so *so* sorry for what happened to your brother, but—"

"You don't have to be sorry anymore. You can create a future where there's nothing to be sorry about. Where Etan and the others are still alive, and you aren't in prison here . . . Or *here,*" she said, tapping him gently on the forehead with her finger.

"Please believe me," Kyle said. "I would do anything, truly *anything,* to fix what I did. But I think we both know you're suggesting something that's not possible."

"Listen to me," she said, her eyes growing stern. "You took away my brother and you are going to help me bring him back."

Perhaps humoring her was the kindest thing Kyle could do right now. He accepted this, deciding that the next time she asked to visit, he would simply decline. For the moment, he would play along. "So, what do I do, jump in a spaceship, turn the clock back to that morning, fly in a different direction and then everything just turns out okay?"

"It's not that simple, I'm afraid," she said. "If you went back to the day of the crash, there'd be two of you there. It'd be too risky." The way she answered him seemed so rational and automatic.

"Risky how?" Kyle asked.

Myrna looked a little frazzled by the question. "I don't know exactly," she said curtly. "It just would be."

"So what do I do?" he asked, humoring her.

"You need to go to your father, before he was your father. You'll go to early 1998—right before you were born. Tell him as little as you can, but tell him enough to make sure that, whatever happens, he stops you from getting into a car on the morning of March 13, 2014. That's it," she said. "I know your relationship with your father is spotty—"

"Spotty doesn't begin to describe it," Kyle said, feeling the slightest bit of regret for sending his father off so harshly earlier. "So, I have to convince a guy who failed me my whole life that in *sixteen* years, the son he's going to abandon is going to need his help on this one particular day? What do I tell him to do? Steal my car keys?"

"I'm hesitant to suggest an exact course of action for him," she said. "Simply by sending you back to 1998, things may change enough by 2014 where too specific a plan could become useless. Your father's just going to have to think on his feet."

"Why does it have to be him? What about my mother?" he asked. "Can't she help us instead?"

Myrna looked away from Kyle. For the first time, her confidence seemed less than one-hundred percent. "I'm told that she's not a good candidate for this," she said. "That's all I know . . . "

In the course of five minutes, Kyle had gone from feeling bad for Myrna to being totally engrossed in every word she was speaking. There was nothing Kyle wouldn't give for the chance to change what happened on the day of the crash. And, here was someone telling him that maybe he could.

"So, let's say it works . . . " Kyle said. "Then what?"

"If you convince your father in 1998 to do what you need him to in 2014, then when you leave him in '98 and come back to 2016, everything should be better."

"Just like that?" Kyle said.

Myrna nodded. "My brother and those other kids will still be alive, and you won't be in prison."

Kyle almost smiled and then whispered to himself. "Wouldn't that be something?"

"Just be careful," she said. "You don't want to do anything when you go back that's going to have unintended consequences. You could really mess up 2016 if you're not careful in 1998. Think of the butterfly effect."

Kyle had never heard the term before and squinted at her.

Myrna rolled her eyes. She lifted her hand and held her pointer finger out to the side. "Pretend my finger is this year, and that there's an invisible line extending out from my finger forever. That invisible line is everything after this year."

Kyle nodded.

She still held up her finger, but now pushed it slightly with her other hand, changing its angle in the air. "Now imagine that some tiny change moves my finger just the teeniest bit. It wouldn't affect this year very much, and maybe not even next year, but eventually that invisible line is going to be further and further from the original line. Eventually, even the tiniest thing—like the flapping of a butterfly's wings—can have a major impact on the future."

"So, if I do this, I'm actually coming back to a different world," Kyle said.

"They would say, a different 'timestream,'" Myrna answered. "It's the same world, just with an alternate history."

"Who's 'they'?" Kyle asked.

"If you present this to your father properly in 1998," she said, ignoring his question, "come 2014, he'll be as eager to make things right with you, as you are eager to change the fate of those kids."

"If I say 'okay', what happens next?" Kyle asked. "Where's the time machine?"

"I'm not entirely sure how they're going to get the silk blot to you," she said. "But you'll know it when you see it. That's how you time weave."

"Silk blot?" Kyle asked. The more details she gave him, the crazier it all sounded, but it also became harder to imagine that she was making it all up.

"I believe you just, kind of, go inside of it," she said. "You'll figure it out."

"Wait, you've never done this before," he said, smiling as he realized it.

"I tried," she said. "I couldn't."

"You couldn't? What does that mean? What makes you think *I* can?" he asked.

"You'll know pretty quickly," Myrna answered. "For those without the right genetic predisposition, it's nearly impossible."

"Genetic predisposition?"

"It's like tongue rolling, or ear wiggling," Myrna said. "Some people can travel back—or forward—without feeling the same physical effects most of us do. You'll know right away if you're not one of them."

"And what if I'm not one of the lucky ones?" Kyle asked.

"You have a lot of questions," she said. "I understand. Unfortunately, I don't have any more answers."

"It sounds risky," he said.

"Are you so in love with the way things have worked out that you're not willing to try to change them, even if there's some risk?" she asked.

Kyle sat speechless, considering everything. If she was crazy, it didn't matter what he thought. But, what if this was real?

"You're a child-killer, and I'm giving you the chance *not* to be. Take this," she said, handing him an envelope which he quickly stuck into his pants, before the guards could see. "There's three-hundred dollars in there. All of the bills are from earlier than 1998. Get yourself a hotel room when you go back."

This was so much to take in. "What if my father doesn't believe me?"

"Do you believe *me*?" Myrna asked.

"I'm not sure," Kyle answered. "Maybe."

"Then, it's possible . . . A lot of people's lives depend on you succeeding, including your own," she said. "Unless you consider being locked up in here *a life* . . .

"Oh! Timeline," she continued. "You've got forty-eight hours. After that, the silk blot will expire and it won't work to get you back. Also, when you want to come back, you have to enter the silk blot in the same exact place you exited . . . And, do not bring anyone else back with you. That's the last thing we need."

"What if it takes me longer than forty-eight hours?"

Myrna smiled impatiently. "You have one job—one conversation you need to have. You have to understand that the timestream is like a life form of its own—it's looking to survive. It's resistant to change, and it's not welcoming to uninvited guests. The longer you stay in that time, where you don't belong, the more you'll find things trying to push you out. You don't want to be there any longer than you have to."

Myrna stood up, and put her hand on Kyle's shoulder. "Keep your eye out. You'll know the silk blot when you see it. We only get one chance at this."

CHAPTER 6

THREE DAYS HAD PASSED SINCE MYRNA'S VISIT and . . . nothing.

Kyle felt nervous that perhaps he'd failed to notice the mysterious silk blot she'd told him was coming. He now felt invested enough in the idea of going back that he was hoping Myrna was not just a crazy lady. At the same time, he didn't *really* expect anything to happen. But since her visit, he felt more alive than he had in years. He was grasping onto the hope Myrna had brought him, even if it sounded completely insane.

"You remind me of this dog I once had, Cuatro,"

Ochoa said. "Waiting. Shifting. All nervous and shit. What the fuck is up with you?"

"What kind of name is that for a dog?" Kyle asked. "Four?"

"Before we trained him up right, he sent four people to the emergency room," Ochoa said. "Seriously, what's up, bro?"

"Nothing. Really," Kyle said.

"I don't believe you," Ochoa said. "Normally, you're all chill and shit. Right now, it's like you know something, and you ain't telling. You're on the edge man—and it's putting me on the fuckin' edge."

Radbourn tapped his keys on the metal door as he opened it. "Bunk check," he said, pushing open the door of their cell. He walked in and started casually looking around. He moved closer to Ochoa's bed to look underneath, craning his neck to see.

Ochoa lifted up his heavy, metal bunk with one

hand. "Save your back, Rad. I ain't got shit under there."

Radbourn stood up. "Thank you, Trevor," he said, eyeing the empty floor underneath. Now, Ochoa went over to Kyle's side and did the same. The beds had to be almost 200 pounds, and Ochoa lifted them almost effortlessly.

"Pizza night tonight, boys. We put an extra guard in the mess hall 'cause too many of you little fuckers can't keep your hands off other guys' food." He smiled as he nodded in the general direction of their cell, signifying that his quick once over was good enough. "You faggots make sure you keep your hands to yourselves." Rad walked out of their cell and slammed the gate shut. "Gotta love pizza night. See ya when I see ya, boys."

Kyle laid down again, hoping he might be able to get a little more rest.

"Is somebody fucking with you and makin' you all nervous?" Ochoa asked. "'Cause all you have to do is tell me."

"No one fucks with me," Kyle answered.

"Yeah, I know," Ochoa answered with a laugh. "I wonder why that is." Kyle's experience at Stevenson Youth would've been very different if he hadn't been bunked with the scariest looking guy in the whole facility.

Kyle listened as Ochoa hissed through a round of pushups on the floor between their beds. "Ewww . . . " he said, getting to his feet after twenty-five or thirty reps.

Kyle looked down and nearly did a double take. As if from thin air, he noticed a fairly large puddle next to Ochoa. It definitely hadn't been there before. Kyle looked up at the ceiling, but there was no leak above them, nor was there a water source flowing nearby. *This might be it*, he thought, as his heart began to thump in his chest.

Kyle hopped off of his bed and knelt down beside to the puddle.

Ochoa hissed through his teeth. "The fuckin'

toilet's leakin' again. Those assholes won't fix it until there's kaka coming up."

Kyle reached down and dipped his finger into the puddle.

Ochoa scrunched up his face. "What the hell?"

Kyle pulled his finger from the liquid and looked at it. He knew immediately that this was it. The black, viscous material was thicker than water, more like a jelly. "This is what I've been waiting on," he said, without looking at Ochoa.

"You've lost it, white boy," Ochoa said with a quick laugh.

Kyle carefully lifted the oval shape from under its edge like he was peeling off a label. He held the silk blot in front of him and tried to look through it, but all he could see was deep black. It was sort of like a fabric, but it was liquidy too. He waved his hand behind the silk blot, but he couldn't see through.

Ochoa wasn't laughing now. "What the fuck

is that?" he asked, grabbing at it to try to get a better look.

"Be careful, Och,'" Kyle said.

Kyle stuck his finger inside, and watched it disappear, as if he were poking wet sand at the beach. Ochoa sidled up next to Kyle and stuck his finger in more aggressively, then his whole hand. "What the fuck is this shit, Kyle?"

Now, Kyle was smiling. He pulled the silk blot toward him and pressed his forehead into the form, allowing the whole crown of his head to enter the strange abyss.

"Tell me if you can hear me," he said to Ochoa, and then Kyle closed his eyes and pressed his whole head inside. "Och! Och! Can you hear me?" Kyle couldn't hear a thing, except an echo of his own voice. He opened his eyes, but it was pitch black in there with no light source.

Kyle pulled his head out. "Did you hear anything?"

He saw a gleam in Ochoa's eyes. "I didn't hear

nothing. But, look bro. It's stretching," Ochoa said. What had started out the size of a large pancake was now morphing into something the size of a pizza pie.

"What's in there, bro?" Ochoa asked. "Let's go all the way in."

Myrna had told Kyle he needed to go alone. He had to try to see if there was some combination of words that could dissuade Ochoa.

"You can't, Och'," Kyle said.

Ochoa smiled like he always did when Kyle said something he disagreed with. "I can't? Watch me, bro."

Kyle put his hand firmly on his shoulder to stop him. "Dude. This is important."

"What is it?" Ochoa asked.

Kyle took a deep breath. He couldn't think of any words that would make Ochoa *not* want to join him. "I can't tell you. I have to go, but I'll be back soon. Just stay here, Och. Please, stay here."

"Aight, bro," Ochoa said. Kyle was glad he was being reasonable.

Kyle gave Ochoa a fist-bump, and then lifted the silk blot on top of himself and drew it over his head like he was putting on a shirt. Once his entire top half was inside, he lifted one leg up and in, then the other. It was a strange sensation to pass through something, but still feel like he was holding it in his hand. The silk blot felt much heavier now. Like carrying a twenty-pound pancake.

Kyle immediately bumped his head on something. He reached up with one hand and felt a curved metal ceiling right above him. He was in some kind of enclosed tunnel. He had the sensation he was on an incline as well. Between the darkness, the weight of the silk blot, and the uneven ground, he needed to drop to his hands and knees to find his balance.

As his eyes began to slightly adjust, Kyle saw U-shaped handles on the floor in front of him. The tunnel sloped upward ahead of him. He looked behind him and could see the handles continue downward far into the darkness.

"What the hell is this, bro?" Ochoa asked as he crawled up from behind Kyle. "It's crazy hot in here."

Kyle should've known better than to think he could just ask his cellmate to let him have this to himself.

"Seriously, Och, it isn't safe for you to be here," Kyle said. "You've gotta go back."

Ochoa ignored him. "Damn, this place needs some air conditioning. It's so hot, it's hard to breathe," he said.

"You serious, Och?" Kyle asked. "I don't feel hot at all."

"This feels like being locked in a hot car on ninety-five degree day," Ochoa said. "My uncle did that to me and my brother once. Forgot all about us. I think this is even hotter though."

Kyle realized that a little bit of light was radiating out from the silk blot. It had been black before, but now seemed to glow with the same dim, fluorescent tone of the lights at Stevenson Youth Correctional. As Kyle pulled himself up toward the next rung, he wondered why Ochoa felt so hot in the tunnel and he didn't.

About fifteen minutes later, they reached a rung that was larger and had ridges running across it. Kyle brought his face closer. He groaned, pulling the heavy silk blot up for light. Etched into the rung was the year *2015*. They appeared to be climbing back in time.

Kyle kept crawling along, slowly moving from rung to rung. Behind him, Ochoa was huffing and puffing. The tunnel *was* cramped, and pulling the heavy silk blot up the incline wasn't easy, but even by the dim light of the silk blot, Kyle could tell Ochoa was struggling so much more than he was to pull himself to each successive rung. It was another fifteen minutes or so of climbing uphill before Kyle reached another large rung with ridges. This one read *2014*.

"How we doin', Och?" Kyle called out.

"You think . . . we're still . . . in the facility?" Ochoa called ahead faintly, unable to catch his breath. "I need to get out of here real soon."

Kyle waited for Ochoa to catch up and pulled the silk blot up between their faces. "Och, we're not in Stevenson anymore."

Ochoa just looked at him and breathed heavily. Kyle sat on one of the smaller rungs, happy to take a break if his friend needed it.

"If we ain't in Stevenson, then are you gonna tell me what's goin' on?" Ochoa asked, a hint of fear in his voice. "I think maybe we should turn back."

"Can't do that, Och," Kyle said. "C'mon, just follow me."

CHAPTER 7

FEBRUARY 3, 1998

eighteen years earlier

"WE'RE HERE," KYLE CALLED OUT. HE COULD hear Ochoa clanging up the tunnel behind him, but it had been a long time since his friend had caught his breath enough to speak. There was no question Ochoa was faster, stronger and in better shape than Kyle. Kyle again wondered why he was having such a hard time, and thought about what Myrna had said about genetic predisposition. Maybe Kyle was like someone who could wiggle his ears and Ochoa wasn't.

Almost five hours after climbing into the tunnel, they were finally approaching the large rung which read *1998*. By now, Kyle's eyes had adjusted and he could see the numbers clearly. "This is it," Kyle said.

"Thank God," Ochoa whispered, barely able to get the words out.

Kyle was relieved that his friend had made it at all. There were moments during the journey when he wasn't sure he would. It seemed that as each hour passed, Ochoa's body started to give out on him more and more. Eventually, a loud groan accompanied each movement Ochoa made as he climbed through the tunnel. Behind him, Kyle heard a regular pattern of "ugh . . . ugh . . . ugh . . . ugh," before Ochoa finally reached a point, between the rungs for *2004* and *2003*, when he curled himself into a ball along the curved wall and just refused to move. After stopping for fifteen minutes in the passageway, Kyle had to call his bluff by starting to move on without him. Thirty seconds later, Ochoa was on the move again, the ugh-ughing soundtrack continuing for the remainder of their trip.

"How, ugh . . . do we get, ugh . . . out?" Ochoa

gasped as he caught up with Kyle. He hadn't spoken much in over an hour. "So thirsty."

Kyle pulled the silk blot up to the opening right above the rung. It looked like the slot on a vending machine where you insert a dollar bill, but much larger. "Just help me try to feed this thing into the hole," Kyle said. The two boys lifted their exhausted arms, trying to steady the blot, one grabbing at each end. They fed the blot partially into the slot, but nothing happened.

"Rest," Ochoa said. "I gotta rest."

Both boys let go of the silk blot, which hung out from the slot right under the 1998 rung.

"Why's it say 1998?" Ochoa asked.

"That's where we are," Kyle said. "If I can just get us out of here." For a second, Kyle considered the idea that this could be some kind of trick. Some measure of revenge cooked up by the families of the kids from Bus #17.

Kyle pulled himself up to look at the slot, but fell forward. Before he even noticed what was happening, his top half was inside the silk blot. Hanging it in the slot had been exactly right! He reached his arm through and pulled Ochoa by the shirt.

"Mutherfucker!" Ochoa said, panting. "You *did* break us out."

Myrna had said not everyone could physically handle traveling through time. Kyle sensed that Ochoa might have gotten through it by virtue of his elite fitness, but wondered whether he could even survive the trip back. Nevertheless, unless this *was* some elaborate trick, they were about to step outside into the year 1998. *Really step back into 1998!* Kyle's head was spinning with the revelation that time travel—or time weaving, as Myrna called it—actually existed. *How come more people don't know about this?* he wondered, just as he poked his head out of the silk blot.

The moment Kyle's eyes came through the silk blot, he was hit by blinding sunlight and the blaring noise from a machine. It sounded like a lawnmower.

He took a few seconds to get his bearings as several images attacked his brain at once.

Kyle stepped forward and froze instinctively. He pulled his foot back just before he stepped out into a huge empty space in front of him. Ochoa appeared next to him. "Don't move," Kyle said. "And don't look down."

Ochoa looked wobbly on his feet and Kyle wasn't sure what to do. They were standing on a narrow metal crossbeam, at least three stories above an active construction site. The lawnmower noise was actually a bulldozer down below, pushing a load of dirt into a huge mound. They were on the skeleton of an unfinished six—or seven-story building.

They were the only ones standing on the structure, but there was plenty of activity below them. Kyle spotted a case of water bottles sitting on the crossbeam about twenty feet away. "Stay here, Och."

Kyle took his time and walked sideways, moving

carefully across the horizontal beam and holding onto vertical ones when they were within reach. He carefully bent down and picked up a bottle of water.

When Kyle got back to him, Ochoa was sitting on the beam, his legs dangling off, staring into space. Two nearby cranes swung metal plates toward the other side of the building.

Ochoa guzzled the entire bottle of water in one sip. He was panting like a dog. Kyle heard the water come right back up before he saw it come out of Ochoa's mouth. Kyle watched the vomit fall about forty feet down, thankfully out of the way of any of the workers below. Ochoa had a concerned look on his face. He was a guy who didn't run up against physical limitations very often. And, even though Kyle had simply felt like moving through the tunnel was on par with a tough workout, for some reason it had been much, much more difficult for his friend.

Kyle looked around, trying to gauge their

options. He could see enough of the skyline to know undeniably where they were. "You're gonna be alright, Och," he said.

He picked up the silk blot from the beam and was relieved to feel that it didn't weigh much at all. It felt as light as it had in Kyle's cell before he and Ochoa went inside of it.

Kyle knew it wouldn't take be before one of the construction guys down below noticed the two boys in khaki prison scrubs hanging out on their half-finished building. There were ladders going down to ground level, but they'd have to cross several beams to get there. "Let's go, Och."

Kyle led the way, but made sure to keep far enough away from Ochoa, who still looked shaky, so that he wouldn't reflexively grab him if he lost his balance. When Kyle reached the ladder, he turned to watch Ochoa. He could see his friend making very slow progress, the combination of fear and exhaustion weighing heavily on him. "Maybe try not to look down, Och," Kyle said.

Ironically, it was when Ochoa took his eyes off of his feet that he had a problem. He made a messy step and lost his balance. He was close enough to grab a vertical beam as he started to go down, but his legs were dangling off the building. Kyle watched in horror as Ochoa slid down the beam, legs flailing. He caught himself by grabbing onto the horizontal beam and clung to the intersection of the two beams like a baby koala. He panicked and closed his eyes. Most people wouldn't have had the upper body strength to catch the beam like Ochoa had, much less hang suspended there.

"Och!" Kyle screamed. "Look here. Look at me."

Ochoa opened his eyes into slits, and looked down.

"Here! Not down," Kyle snapped, holding on to a vertical beam. "Now, listen to me . . . You're gonna be fine. You've just got to pull your leg up over the beam you're holding onto . . . "

Ochoa shook his head fast. Kyle had never seen him look scared like this. "I can't. If I try, I'm gonna fall . . . My hands are slipping."

Kyle carefully walked over to him and knelt down. "You're not gonna fall." He wrapped his left arm around the vertical beam, trying to secure himself. Now, he reached his right hand down to Ochoa.

"It's not gonna work," Ochoa said. "I have no strength right now."

"Look at me," Kyle said. "How many times have you saved my ass?"

The panic on Ochoa's face lowered by a degree or two. "A few times."

"Then just listen to me and let me help you," Kyle said, "I got you, Och."

Ochoa grabbed Kyle's hand. For a second, Kyle felt overburdened by Ochoa's weight and felt himself sliding off the building. But, Kyle pulled hard against the vertical beam and was able to provide enough support for Ochoa to get himself up into a position straddling the horizontal beam. Still holding onto the vertical beam, Kyle gave Ochoa his hand again and helped him steady himself as he stood up. "Fuck, bro," Ochoa said. "I almost died right there."

They made it the rest of the way down the side of the building without further incident. They hustled unnoticed through the groups of construction workers moving around at ground level and got out to the street.

Ochoa followed closely behind Kyle. "Something doesn't feel right, bro," he said. "My eyes are all blurry and I have a crazy headache. And I feel all weird inside."

"We've had a really active day, Och. It'll pass," Kyle said, even though he had no idea if that was true. Kyle felt fine. Maybe even *stronger* than he had before they entered the silk blot. He wished his friend had listened and not followed him, but now that he had, getting Ochoa back to 2016 safely had become another critical goal for Kyle.

When they reached the street corner, Kyle stopped for a second and put his hands against the chain-link fence surrounding the construction site. He looked up and confirmed what he was mostly sure of already. "West 28th Street and 11th Avenue," Kyle said. "I wonder if all these construction guys are asking themselves why the hell they're building a prison on some of the most expensive real estate in New York City."

"This is Stevenson right here . . . ?"

"Yeah, it is, Och. Welcome to 1998," Kyle said.

"What the fuck?" Ochoa said. "1998? Like, the year?"

Kyle smiled and put his hand on Ochoa's shoulder. "These guys are building the prison we just broke out of."

Ochoa looked around. He looked down at his own hands, turning them as if he were trying to see if they were real. "But, it doesn't make any sense . . . Nah, man. I don't believe it. It's not possible."

"I don't understand it either, Och," Kyle said. "But we are out here now, right? Instead of in there. So, uh, I say we go with it."

CHAPTER 8

FEBRUARY 3, 1998

later that day

As they passed a newsstand, Kyle took a peek at the cover of *The Daily News*. "February 3, 1998," he said to Ochoa. It looked like every magazine had Bill Clinton and Monica Lewinsky on the cover.

"I'm pretty big for a three-month-old," Ochoa said with a laugh, reminding Kyle that his friend was a few months older than he was. He remembered what Myrna told him about how it was dangerous to time travel within your own life. "Hold on a sec, I gotta take a break."

Ochoa bent over, his hands on his knees. He spoke very deliberately and quietly, gritting his teeth. "If it's 1998, my mama's around. I gotta see her. She's probably up in Washington Heights right now."

"You okay, Och?" Kyle asked. Ochoa was still trying to catch his breath. Kyle saw that his clothes were bubbling off of him, completely drenched with sweat. It looked like he'd gone swimming in them.

"I feel weird," Ochoa said. "All fuzzy and shit. Almost like I'm underwater. And I got this heartbeat in my ears. Real loud."

"Listen, Och," Kyle said. "We've gotta make sure we stick together here. We have to get on the bus up to Flemming in a few hours." He didn't want to say it, but Kyle was afraid he might never see Ochoa again if he let him out of his sight in this condition.

"I gotta see my mom, bro," Ochoa said. "If it's 1998, she ain't dead yet. Not for another five years. I really don't feel good, man. She'll know what to do." Kyle heard the fear inside of every word.

"You absolutely cannot go see your mother, Och," Kyle said. "The lady who sent us here, she said you aren't supposed to go back to a time during your own life. Said it was too dangerous."

Ochoa stopped and took a couple of steps toward the street. "You don't have to come, but I gotta go, bro."

They'd never had a huge disagreement before. Ochoa was stubborn, but picked his battles. "It's a really bad idea, Och. Listen to the words I am saying," Kyle said, grabbing onto Ochoa's shirt. "My guess is that if *you* are standing next to *you* as a baby, something really fucked up is going to happen. That's how that lady made it sound."

"Why are *you* here, then?" Ochoa asked, brushing Kyle's hand away.

Kyle took a deep breath. "I'm here to find my father," he said. "But it's different. Kyle Cash isn't alive in the world we are in right now. Listen, inside Stevenson you always had my back. You've got to trust me to have yours out here. I know you're scared, but trust me!"

"Nah, fuck that. I need my mom," Ochoa said. "Something doesn't feel right. I need to see my mom."

"She won't know you," Kyle said, trying to sound less frustrated than he was. "Don't you get it? To her, the only Trevor Ochoa is the little baby in her stroller."

Ochoa walked into the middle of the street. He turned around to Kyle, pounded his chest and gave him a peace sign. "Mamas always know their children, bro. It's scientifically proven."

"Ochoa," Kyle yelled. "I told you. We gotta stick together."

"Then let's go," Ochoa said, as a car zipped by right in front of him.

Kyle stepped into the street. "Go where?"

"Uptown, bro," Ochoa said. "We'll be careful. I promise."

"You have to follow the rules," Kyle said, chasing

after him. "You can't talk to anyone, or do anything that could change the future. Anything you do could really fuck things up."

"Yeah yeah, I got it," Ochoa said. "The subway's two blocks this way."

"I'm, like, crazy hungry," Ochoa said as they exited the train at 181st Street and St. Nicholas Avenue in Washington Heights. Kyle couldn't argue. They hadn't eaten since breakfast, before their long journey through the tunnel.

"We're in Dominican country, bro," Ochoa said. "But, there's one Puerto Rican restaurant that's off the hook."

"Was it around in 1998?" Kyle asked. He was hungry too, and thought that maybe it was good sign for his health that Ochoa wanted to eat.

"Let's go see," Ochoa said. Kyle saw his friend move with excitement for the first time in a while.

The half hour on an air conditioned train had been good for him. Ochoa still looked shaky, but Kyle could see that he felt energized from being home.

They walked a few blocks and arrived at Salvado's, which was mostly empty, save for a few customers here and there. The hostess sat on a stool, flipping through *The National Enquirer*, not even acknowledging them at first.

"What'd you two do, break out of jail or somethin'?" she asked when she looked up and saw their outfits, with only a hint of a smile.

"No, no, not at all," Kyle said, firing the words out nervously. "We work together. At the hospital."

"Cool," she said. "Which one?" She was a pretty Latina girl with a thick New York accent.

"Crespi Memorial," Kyle answered.

She cocked her eyebrow. "All the way downtown?"

"Best Puerto Rican food in the city," Ochoa said, putting on a charming smile. Kyle had never seen Ochoa flirt with a girl before.

"You think?" she asked. "Why have I never seen you in here, then?"

"It's been a while," Ochoa answered. "I don't live up here no more."

"Blanca," she called to the back. "Table twelve." The hostess brought them to a small table and dropped a couple of menus in front of them. "Blanca's gonna love you," the hostess said with a wink to Kyle as she walked away.

"She was hot, bro," Ochoa said. "I'm not even talkin' about 'I've-been-in-prison-hot.' I'm talkin', real, legit hotness. I'm already lovin' time travel."

"Remember," Kyle said. "We've got to talk to as few people as possible."

"What do you think I'm gonna do—tell her I'm from the future. Probably a good way to get laid, though," Ochoa said with a laugh, standing up. "Be right back. Bathroom."

Kyle barely had a chance to glance at the menu before a tall, attractive blond walked up to the table. She wore an apron over her jean shorts. This must be 'Blanca,' he thought. She was his age—possibly a little younger.

"I'm Allaire," she said, smiling brightly. "I'll be your waitress."

Before Kyle could respond, she sat down in the booth across from him. "Can I sit?" she asked.

"Sure, no prob—" Kyle started to say, but stopped, since she had already sat. A few strands of hair fell into her face and she blew them away, sighing as she did it, and tucking the strands behind her ears. Kyle couldn't take his eyes off of her.

"I thought this would be an easy job. A good way to make some cash," Allaire said. "But, there's this dude, Fernando, in the back. He's such an asshole. He thinks he can do whatever he wants to the girls. Little pervert slapped my ass twice. I told him if he does it again I'll cut his fuckin' hand off. Anyway, I'm just feeling like 'screw it.' Maybe I'll just walk out right now." She was barely taking a breath between sentences. "You're probably hungry, though, right? Do you know what you want?"

"Not really," Kyle answered.

"I'll make it simple," she said. "You like chicken or pork better? You're cute, by the way."

"Uh . . . "

"Get the pork, bro," Ochoa said as he walked back over to the table. "Always the pork."

"Alright I'll bring you both the pork. You're not Jewish, right? Cuz if you are, you should go for the chicken," she said with a laugh. "I'm not hanging out back there in the kitch, though. That jerk can bring it out himself when it's done." She got up to walk away. "I hope that's okay with you guys," she said.

"Uh . . . sure," Kyle answered.

She walked away from their table, while Kyle followed her with his eyes. She was stunning, and had a frantic energy that Kyle wasn't used to. He wasn't really used to any type of female energy these days. As much as he tried to ignore it, every ounce of his being wanted to follow her.

"That waitress is wacky as shit, bro," Ochoa said.

"And what happened to talking to as few people as possible? Mr. I-wrote-the-time-travel rulebook is trying to fuck the waitress and shit before we even—"

"I'm not trying to fuck the waitress," Kyle said. "But, damn . . . " Kyle took a deep breath when his mind shifted back to finding his father. He didn't have a whole lot of time, and this side trip to Washington Heights wasn't helping matters.

"So, I was tryin' to figure it out," Ochoa said. "I think if we knock on the door of the apartment in an hour, my mom'll be home."

"We definitely cannot go up to your apartment," Kyle said. "Remember? You have to trust me. What if she answers the door and she is holding the baby? That's you man!"

"We're at odds again, man, and that's okay," Ochoa said, taking a statement right out of Stevenson Correctional's annual, mandatory conflict resolution class. "I'm great with babies—and my mom will know what to do. You need to trust *me*, bro."

Kyle was getting frustrated that Ochoa wasn't getting the message. "You don't think I want to see my mom again?" Kyle asked. "Tell her not to kill herself when I get sent up to prison? But I can't. I have a job. Have one conversation with one person, and then we get back to 2016. You weren't even supposed to be here, Och."

"Everything happens for a reason though, right?" Ochoa asked.

"I don't know if it does, Och," Kyle answered. He hadn't bought into that way of thinking since before the crash. What reason was there for twelve kids getting killed like they had? "What if we go see your mom, but you just look . . . from across the street, maybe? You just can't talk to her."

"I want to know why I feel so weird," Ochoa said, his voice cracking a bit. "I threw up two more times in the bathroom just now. The second time, there was some blood in it. And my legs feel mad weak."

"I'm honestly not sure what's going on, Och," Kyle said. "The sooner I go find my father, the faster we can get back to Stevenson and get you better . . ."

"Why would we go back?" Ochoa asked.

Kyle wished Ochoa could've heard Myrna. Could've seen her telling Kyle the rules. "Because in forty-eight hours, the silk blot—the thing we went inside to get to the tunnel—it's gonna stop working."

"Well then we've got some time before we have to decide," Ochoa said.

Kyle sighed. He didn't have enough answers to debate Ochoa about this. "After we eat, let's go see your mom. Then, I'll take care of business and we'll get back. But we have to keep our distance," Kyle said. "Deal?"

Ochoa nodded. Kyle hoped he could trust him. And, Kyle hoped he wasn't making a huge mistake.

CHAPTER 9

THE BOYS SAT ON THE STEPS OF A WASHINGTON Heights apartment building across the street from the one Ochoa grew up in. Ochoa was still having trouble on-and-off catching his breath, even though it had been hours since they'd left the tunnel. It was drizzling, and the moisture felt great to Kyle. Something *was* definitely wrong with Ochoa, but Kyle couldn't offer anything more than trying his best to get them back to 2016 quickly.

"You see that swing right there? Second one from the left," Ochoa asked, pointing at the playground inside the housing project complex. "That's how I got this scar right here above my eye. I was five years old, running from the swings to those monkey bars, and WHAM! Maricela Maldonado's swing completely blindsides me. Eight stitches. The amount of blood coming out of my head was crazy. Thought my mom was gonna have a heart attack, bro."

Kyle looked at Ochoa. "You know what else is crazy? That day at the playground hasn't even happened yet. At least not in this version of time."

"That makes my head hurt, bro," Ochoa said. "Hey, why you think you're getting this chance, to go back and try to fix what happened?"

Kyle breathed in deeply. He needed to toe the line and make sure he didn't give Ochoa ammunition to go back on their deal about not approaching his mother. "I honestly don't know. I think a lot of people were hurt when those kids died, and one of them figured out a way to try to fix things."

"Oh shit," Ochoa said. "There's my mom."

Kyle watched an attractive Puerto Rican woman pushing an umbrella stroller up the street toward the apartment building entrance. It was getting close to nine o'clock—four hours until the last bus of the night left for Flemming.

Ochoa stood up. "There she is, bro. She's alive!" Kyle saw tears welling up in his eyes. Ochoa took a few steps forward to the edge of the sidewalk.

"Och!" Kyle called out. "Stop right there . . . Listen, you can't—I mean, the lady who set this up, she warned me about this. I'm serious!" He reached out to grab Ochoa by the shirt, but his friend stiff-armed him away forcefully. "Och, seriously, just—"

Ochoa was in a trance. He started toward his mother, totally ignoring Kyle as he stepped out into the street.

"Dammit, Ochoa!" Kyle shouted, as he walked to the edge of the sidewalk. He looked up into the air, out of moves. He didn't know what to do. "Don't fucking do it, man!"

Ochoa was halfway across the street now. "Veronica Ochoa," he called out. The young woman stopped and turned to him. In the light of the apartment building entrance, Kyle could see the resemblance.

Kyle felt a sense of panic rush over him as he stepped into the street to follow Ochoa. He nearly got hit by a taxi, and was forced to step back and watch from a distance. The light had changed and cars were whizzing by now. Ochoa was approaching his mother, and Kyle stared back at the traffic light, waiting for it to turn red. His new plan was to run full speed at Och and tackle him. The light seemed to stay green forever, and Ochoa was now just a few steps from the stroller. Just as he glanced down at the baby inside, Ochoa suddenly raised his hands to his ears as if he were in great pain.

It was then that Kyle noticed a blond woman about thirty yards down the street from them. She wore a dark baseball cap, and seemed to be as fixed on Ochoa and his mother as Kyle was.

As he watched Ochoa bend down in agony, clutching his head, he saw the woman pull out a gun and aim it toward them. Veronica didn't see her, but started to back away from Trevor as his screams filled the street. Kyle cringed seeing his best friend in so much pain.

The light turned red and Kyle began to run toward Ochoa, "No!" he screamed at the woman with the gun. She looked in his direction, and lowered her weapon, appearing indecisive for a moment.

Just as Kyle was about to reach him, Ochoa's head blew apart like a watermelon that had been hit by a baseball bat. Kyle screamed.

He quickly glanced at the woman with the gun, but she was already running the other way down the street. She definitely hadn't shot Ochoa. It would've taken a powerful shotgun to do that to his head.

Kyle knelt down next to Ochoa's body, his head reduced to a pile of skin and brains. For a moment, Kyle was transported back into the front seat of

Joe's Audi, staring at the mangled head of his best friend.

Meanwhile, Veronica had quickly rushed little Ochoa into their apartment, probably thinking she'd just witnessed a shooting.

Kyle pounded Ochoa's chest. "Dammit!" he shouted. "Shit, Ochoa. Why couldn't you just listen . . . ?" His voice trailed off and Kyle cried for a moment. The emotion of the whole journey flowed out of him. Everything had been tactical to this point and Kyle had been distracted from the significance of what he was embarking on.

He thought about whether there was any way to fix this. *What if I drag him back to 2016?* Kyle wondered. He pulled out the silk blot and tried to stuffing Ochoa's hand inside. The silk blot reacted differently now. The material held firm, instead of swallowing his hand like before. He thought back to his conversation with Myrna, and remembered she said he had to enter and exit the silk blot in the same place. There was no way he was getting

Ochoa back to the unfinished prison building. *How can I make this okay?* he thought, panicking. *What can I do?*

When the sirens began, Kyle stood up. He had no identification. If he was there when the cops came, all bets were off. He could spend the next forty-eight hours in police custody if they thought he had something to do with Ochoa's death. Then he'd never stop the crash, or make it back to 2016. He quickly assessed that the best chance to save the lives of the kids on the bus, and for all he knew, maybe even Ochoa's, was to leave right away. He bent down once more to put Ochoa's hands gently across his chest. Then Kyle ran in the direction of the subway station.

CHAPTER 10

KYLE RAN FOR AS LONG AS HE COULD BEFORE slowing down to a fast walk on 181st Street. He was about two short blocks from the train and felt like his chest was going to implode if he didn't take a break. He also desperately needed replacements for his old, prison-issued canvas slippers.

The image of Ochoa's head blowing apart, clear off his neck, kept running through Kyle's head. If he failed to stop the bus crash now, Ochoa would have died for nothing. He had to try to think of something else—anything at all.

"Hey!" a voice called out behind him.

Instinctively, Kyle turned. It was the chatty

waitress standing in front of Salvado's, the restaurant he'd eaten at with Ochoa just a couple of hours ago. She was smoking a cigarette while she read a magazine.

"You're still dressed like some kind of mental patient," she called out.

Kyle turned and gave her a polite smile, but he didn't stop. In another time, in another universe, he would've been all over the opportunity to talk to her. She was the kind of girl he always liked—soft looking with a mischievous streak.

Having caught his breath, he started jogging in the direction of the train station.

A few seconds later, he heard footsteps closing in on him, and then a hand on his shoulder. He knew it was her. "Hey! You're rude, you know that?"

"I'm sorry," he said, irritated that he had to stop again. "Look, I'm in a hurry."

"Where ya goin'?" she asked.

"I gotta catch the train."

"Downtown?" she asked. "I just heard one pass. So you're looking at another twenty minutes. Don't bother hustling."

"Thanks," he said, still not stopping.

"Where's your buddy, the Sasquatch?" she asked.

Kyle stopped and took a breath. "Don't call him that."

She wrinkled her brow. "Uh . . . Sorry."

He felt a hitch on the inside. If he let himself, he would start sobbing right here. "He's somewhere good, I hope."

"Okay, weirdo," she answered.

"Have a good night," Kyle said, starting toward the train again.

"Hey, wait up," she said. "Lemme get my jacket. I'm going that way too." She ran in the direction of the restaurant.

Kyle thought about ignoring her, but if she was right about the train time, then he was just going to see her up on the tracks again anyway.

She went inside the restaurant and was out again within thirty seconds.

"Haha," she said. "Good luck finishing service without a waitress!" She laughed to herself and then screamed out "ASSHOLES!" to punctuate the laughter.

"So, what are you in such a hurry for?" she asked. She shrugged when he ignored the question.

"You remember my name?" she asked, tucking her arm under his. "Allaire Thompson . . ."

He liked watching her lips move, and imagined kissing them. He didn't need a distraction like this right now, but he couldn't help himself. "I'm Kyle Cash."

"So, are we, uh, gonna hang out, or what?" she asked.

"I can't," Kyle answered, wishing he'd met her under different circumstances. "I need to catch a bus upstate."

"Back to prison?" she laughed.

Kyle was tongue-tied for a minute. "No!" was all he could manage in response.

"Sorry, but the outfit . . . " she said again, letting him off the hook with a laugh. She carried herself as confidently as anyone he'd ever met. His buddy Joe Stropoli would have described her as "mint." She had shoulder length blond hair, with pieces that fell in front of her face sometimes. Just the way she softly blew the strands away was sexy. Kyle found it distracting to be near her, and he couldn't help but try to glance at her chest, or steal a look at her butt. He could only imagine how amazing she'd look in a bathing suit . . . or less.

They reached the subway turnstile and Allaire pulled out her Metrocard. Kyle pulled a twenty from the envelope Myrna had given him. She swiped herself through.

Kyle saw the token booth was empty and there was no Metrocard vending machine.

"This time of night," Allaire called out, "you

gotta have your fare ready, Kyle Cash. C'mon, I'll swipe you through."

Kyle shrugged and walked to the turnstile.

"Know what? Keep it," she said.

Kyle considered declining her offer, but swiped himself through and pocketed the fare card.

Kyle stood up as the train approached 42nd Street. He'd let her do most of the talking on the train, since he wasn't about to reveal why he was here. It was the first time he'd had a conversation with a girl his own age since before the bus crash. Not being able to speak about what had just happened to Ochoa forced him to draw his mind away from his grief.

"I've never been to Flemming," she said, standing up with him, grabbing his arm for balance.

Kyle breathed deeply. He looked at her and couldn't believe he had to find a way to ditch her. "It was great meeting you," he said. "But . . . "

"This is what happens every time," she said.

"Am I dumb? Do I have bad breath? Is it my teeth? I know they're a little crooked."

"You're perfect," Kyle said. And he meant it. "I just have some pretty heavy stuff to do when I get upstate . . . It's been great talking—"

"—Don't you want to get to the part where we *stop* talking?" she asked, raising her eyebrows.

Most of the off-the-charts hot girls he'd known tended to play it coy. Kyle was more of a "friend zone" candidate to the Allaires of the world—the stoner nice guy. She wasn't like anyone he'd ever met. It was as if there was nothing she wouldn't say if it came into her head, and because of that, he felt his guard lowering, something he knew he couldn't allow to go too far.

Everything that had gone wrong so far had been the result of Ochoa sneaking into the time tunnel. But, if Kyle let Allaire get on the bus with him, he would be intentionally going against what Myrna had told him to do. He could feel himself wavering already. He was afraid he'd tell Allaire everything if they spent enough time together. She was the kind of girl who made you forget which was left, and which was right.

"Okay, but once we get to Flemming . . . " he started.

Allaire contorted her face. "Okay," she said, imitating him in a nerdy voice, "but once we get to Flemming . . . "

"I guess we're doing this," Kyle said as the train door opened.

Allaire stood on her tip toes and kissed him on the cheek. "Damn right we are."

CHAPTER 11

the next morning

KYLE OPENED HIS EYES WHEN HE FELT ALLAIRE poking his ribs.

The sun was starting to come up just as the bus pulled into Flemming station, a converted barn that was one of the small town's most iconic sites.

"Sorry," he said. "I must've passed out. How long was I asleep?"

"About an hour, but it was nice," she said. "I was just watching you. You're a peaceful sleeper, Kyle Cash." It was jarring that she seemed so invested in him already, but he also loved the way it felt when she was affectionate. "And this new outfit is hot!" she said, of the Polo shirt, Hilfiger jeans and steel-toed Dr. Martens she'd picked out for him during a midnight blitz through Times Square on their way to the Port Authority bus terminal. He'd also gotten himself a two layer, waterproof Columbia jacket, the warmest he could find to combat the freezing temperature.

During the long ride, he had been tempted to share everything with her—the burden of what he'd done to land in prison and the chance to fix things by traveling through time, but he hadn't. Instead, he learned about her life—alcoholic, out-of-the-picture mom, doctor father residing on a tall pedestal in her heart. She was taking some time off from school, living with friends and working as a waitress to support herself. He wasn't sure where taking a four-and-a-half hour bus ride with a stranger fit into her plans, but he'd enjoyed the company.

They exited the bus onto the station's rocky parking lot and Kyle knew it was time to really say "goodbye."

"So what's your plan now?" he asked.

She smiled shyly at him and he could tell that she was hurt. They'd made out a little bit on the bus, and she'd definitely opened up to him. Kyle wished he could offer her something more than "goodbye." He didn't want to part ways either.

"Let me come with you," she said, as if the idea had just struck her in that very moment. "Introduce me to your family."

"Let me buy your ticket back," Kyle said.

"I don't need you to buy me off," she said, blowing her bangs out of her face in a way that made Kyle want to pull her against his body. "Just tell me when I can see you again."

He looked at the ground. "I don't know. There's a lot you don't—"

She put her hands on his cheeks. "This, right here, you and me? This feels right, doesn't it? And we can't ignore that. The universe doesn't make mistakes."

"We just met," Kyle said. "You're great, but—"

"Exactly! We just met, and already it's, like, amazing. And, I think you know too. There's no such thing as a coincidence, Kyle Cash. If I know anything, it's that."

He hated the look on her face right now. How could she be so self-confident, but also so vulnerable? Also, crazy as it was, why did he feel like she was right?

He tapped his pants pocket. "I have your number. I'll call you the next time I'm in the city." He knew it was a lame response.

She shook her head slowly, as if she had some special insight that he didn't, but was going to let him do it his way. With a peck on the lips, she turned and headed inside toward the ticket window. Kyle set off on foot in the direction of Crespi Memorial Hospital.

As a young kid, Kyle used to quiz his mother endlessly about his father. It wasn't until he was a teenager that he realized how painful it must have been for her—having to recall tiny details to share with her son about the man who left them high and dry. He knew, for instance, that Sillow had worked as an orderly in the cardiac ward at Crespi Memorial Hospital before running off to Florida with his new family.

Kyle felt nervous as he took the elevator up to the fourth floor's cardiac wing. What could he possibly tell his father to make him believe? Myrna had told him to share as little as possible. But what could he say to compel a man who'd never bothered with him at all to take action sixteen years from now?

Kyle sat down in the family waiting area and picked up a magazine, pretending to read. It was almost an hour before he heard the pretty receptionist speaking to a man pushing a cart with various tubes and tools on it. He stopped by her counter to talk. "Shave duty, eh, Sillow?" she asked him.

Kyle's father wore dark blue scrubs from head to toe. He leaned over the high counter and moved his face close to hers. "Closest shave since Jack the Ripper, at your service," he answered with a laugh. "Y'know, some of these guys I shave, I think to myself 'you ain't gettin' out of here too soon, buddy.' But, y'know, these old-timers, they want what they want."

The receptionist laughed politely, as if they'd had this exchange a thousand times before. "You just be careful with those sharp objects now, ya hear?"

"Always, Wanda, Always," he said, and then lowering his voice: "I may have a sharp object for you if you're interested."

Wanda laughed, "You are bad!"

Kyle's heart pounded at the sight of his father. He opened his mouth to call out to him, but before he could, Sillow went through a double door labeled "NO ADMITTANCE."

It was nearly an hour before Kyle saw Sillow again. This time, he was talking to another male employee. He passed through one set of doors, and was about to go through another when Kyle called out his name.

Sillow turned and looked at him, cocking an eyebrow. "Yeah? You got a relative in here?"

"No, I uh . . . I was hoping I could buy you lunch," Kyle said. "There's something I want to discuss with you."

"Huh?" Sillow asked, cocking his brow.

"Anywhere you'd like," Kyle said.

"What do you want to do that for?" Sillow asked. "I don't even know you."

"I need to talk to you," Kyle answered.

"Go 'head then," Sillow answered.

"It's probably better if we talk in private," Kyle answered.

Sillow cracked a smile, and looked around, as if someone was putting him on. "I don't know what the hell your deal is, kid, but if you ain't a guest of the hospital, you best get the hell out of here right now."

Kyle tried to think quickly. He leaned in and put on a deadly serious face. "You really don't want me to say what I have to say with all of your coworkers around," he said, hoping to appeal to Sillow's sense of pride.

"Oh, okay, I think I know what this is about," Sillow said. Kyle wondered if there was some way Sillow *did* know. Sillow stepped back and looked up, as if were considering something. "You wanna buy me lunch? Sure, alright. Sizzler down the street. I'll see you there in fifteen minutes."

Kyle stood outside of Sizzler, again trying to push the image of Ochoa's final moments out of his head. He only had a little more than twenty-four hours left to make it back to the construction site in Manhattan before the silk blot closed. Plenty of time if he could make a convincing case to his father.

Just as he began to wonder whether Sillow

might not show up, he saw him headed his way. Sillow flicked his cigarette into the bushes lining the restaurant and moved quickly toward Kyle. Without a word, Sillow grabbed him by the throat, and pushed him back against the brick wall of the restaurant.

"You come see me at work!" he said angrily. "At work? How you think I'm ever gonna settle up if I can't earn a living?"

Kyle tried to wiggle away, but Sillow had him pinned. "You've got it wrong! That's not why I'm here."

"Your one of Kendrick's boys, huh?" Sillow asked. "Well, I don't need some fuckin' kid comin' to my job to remind me to take care of my debts."

"Let me explain," Kyle said. "You've got it wrong."

"You tell him, I'm doin' the best I fuckin' can. I make ten bucks an hour. Tell him I said that owing him doesn't give him the right to send nobody to my work."

"Hold on!" Kyle said. He searched for something he could say to make Sillow back off.

"I see you, or anyone else, here again, they're gonna get it a lot worse than this," Sillow said, and then immediately reared back and delivered a hard blow to Kyle's cheek. For a wiry guy, his father's punch packed a ton of power. Kyle fell back against the wall stunned. Sillow spit onto the concrete next to Kyle barely missing the new shoe on his right foot. Then, he turned to walk away. "Tell him I'll come see him as soon as I got his money."

Kyle couldn't let another day pass without making some headway. He had to get through to his father. And if Sillow wouldn't hear him out with a friendly approach, he'd have to try something different.

CHAPTER 12

KYLE PRESSED THE SLEEVE OF HIS COAT AGAINST his cheek as he walked down Main Street. It had been two years since Kyle had walked through Flemming's downtown district. Amazingly, all but a few of the businesses he remembered from 2014 were "still" around in 1998. He noticed tiny changes, like Kenny's hadn't yet changed the color of its entire exterior from green to maroon, and the underwear on the mannequins in the window of Miss Mabel's Intimates didn't look quite as yellowed and sun damaged yet.

Searching his mind for a way to get Sillow to listen to him, he passed the town's only shooting range, *Ready, Aim, Flemming.* Pointing a gun at Sillow would probably get him to listen, but it would take him more time than he could spare to get a permit—not to mention that he didn't have any identification. *There was no way,* he thought. *Unless . . .*

About a mile down Main Street, on the opposite side, was Dankert Library. It was one of the few large buildings in Flemming, with four white columns, and a huge green door.

He pulled open the heavy door and stepped inside. Kyle was glad to get out of the brisk afternoon chill, and into the warm library. The lobby was lined with glass display cases, each one dedicated to a theme. One was Black History month, another for romance novels, and several were devoted to artwork from students at Flemming Elementary.

One glass display case hung higher than the others, right above doors leading from the lobby into the main part of the library. Kyle smiled as he walked up to it. He could always trust his memory, but he was never more glad to confirm the local saying, "Flemming never changes," than he was now.

The artifacts inside the case—from Flemming's small role in the Revolutionary War—included two matching pistols, each with a wooden handle and an iron shaft, mounted to the back wall of the case. Somewhere in the library, there was a key that would make it possible for him to "borrow" one of the artifacts. Unfortunately, he had no idea where.

Kyle camped in the bathroom adjoining the lobby for twenty minutes, crouched with his feet on a toilet, waiting for the library to close. He waited ten more minutes after someone came in to turn off the bathroom lights, just to be safe, and then went back out into the dark lobby.

He slid a bench across the floor as quietly as he could, placed it underneath the Revolutionary War display case, and stepped up onto it. He fiddled with the door of the case, sliding and prying to see if he could bust the lock. He almost cut his finger when he managed to get it underneath the front panel of the case, but if he pulled any harder, the entire pane of glass might shatter in his face.

He needed something hard to break the glass open. He considered using one of his new shoes, but didn't think it could do the trick. He climbed down and sat on the bench thinking. Just then, he heard a noise coming from inside the library. He didn't bother peeking in. Whoever was there, they were supposed to be, and Kyle was not.

He stepped up onto the bench once more, lining his arm up with the glass. He took his shirt off and wrapped it quickly around his elbow. Closing his eyes, Kyle gave the front of the case a huge jab with his elbow. The resulting pop jarred his ears like an explosion. Kyle felt glass shards pepper his neck and face on their way to the floor. The sensation immediately took him back to the bus crash. Hanging upside down, covered with pieces of windshield, watching drops of blood drip from his buddy Joe to the interior roof of the car—that was as powerless as Kyle had ever felt in his life.

Kyle carefully reached into the front of the Revolutionary War display and grabbed one of the pistols. He pulled it out, careful to avoid slicing his arm on the jagged glass still attached to the front panel of the case. The gun was heavier than he would've guessed. Not surprisingly, he heard footsteps running toward him from inside the library now.

Kyle hopped down from the bench, threw his shirt on and ran out of the lobby onto Main Street. He quickly turned a corner and crossed the street, shoving the pistol into the back of his new jeans.

When he reached the huge field behind Silverman High School, he sat on the ground and picked the remaining tiny pieces of glass off of his shirt. He took out the pistol and felt it in his hand.

Except for a short rest on the bus, his adrenaline had been pumping ever since Kyle pushed himself through the silk blot in his prison cell. The workday was over, so he'd have to wait for morning now to confront Sillow if he didn't want to risk going to his apartment and possibly seeing his mother. He laid back in the grass now, worried for the first time that he might've already messed up the future in ways he could never predict. Between Ochoa following him, and being killed, and now, his short relationship with Allaire, he'd definitely gone against what Myrna asked of him. The more Kyle thought about Ochoa's death, the less real it felt. Kyle wondered about the *rules* of time weaving. *Would he come back to a world where Ochoa was alive? If he was successful in stopping the bus crash, and never went to prison, would he even remember Ochoa?*

He turned onto his belly in the grass now, using his arms as a pillow, and quickly drifted into sleep.

Kyle opened his eyes to the sight of Allaire's face four inches from his. Surprised, he sprang up quickly and saw that it was dark out.

"I really *could* watch you sleep forever," she said turning toward him. "Sorry if I freaked you out."

"I was so tired, I didn't even notice," Kyle said. "Why didn't you go back to the city?"

She leaned over and kissed him on the lips, lingering for a moment with her tongue. "Aren't you *glad* I didn't?"

"What have you been doing all day?" he asked. "How'd you find me?"

"Would you believe I spent the whole day at Sam Goody checking out CDs and just happened to bump into you?" she asked.

"No," he said. He looked a few feet past her and saw a shopping bag. "Did you buy a sleeping bag?"

"It's going to dip into the thirties tonight," she said. "Unless you've got a hotel reservation I wasn't aware of."

Kyle had spent a lot of the money Myrna had given him on clothing. He laid back in the grass and winced when he laid on the gun. "What time is it?" he asked, pulling the pistol out from the back of his pants.

"About 7:30," she said. "Is the gun for that man? Does that thing even *work*? When I saw him hit you, I wanted to knock him out. But I was afraid you'd be mad if I interfered . . . Who is he? Are you some kind of badass? Prison clothes, a fight with some stranger . . . It's okay if you are. It's kind of sexy."

"Allaire, what are you doing?" Kyle asked. He wasn't angry. He was flattered, but the longer she stuck around, the more she complicated things.

Now, she climbed on top of him. Her bangs fell

into her face, so she blew them upwards. "Listen, Mister! When I told you I wasn't just going to ignore the clear signs, I wasn't kidding. You and I are here for a reason. This could be the first chapter of our love story. And I don't care whether you're a little freaked out, or a little hesitant, or you're not ready to get on board just yet. That's fine. But, I'm gonna make sure I'm here once you get over yourself."

As tempting as it was not to move an inch, Kyle gently moved Allaire off of him. "You're aware that we barely know each other, right? You don't know anything about me."

"So what? We have all of that learning ahead of us. How exciting is that? Everyone's so concerned about doing things in order," she said. "Why can't we start with all the good stuff and hope for the best? I dare you to prove to me that I'm wrong about you, Kyle Cash. I don't think you can."

Kyle turned to her and put a hand on her knee. "I don't think you understand, Allaire . . . "

"What don't I understand?"

"You're . . . gorgeous. No guy in his right mind *wouldn't* want to hear these things from you."

"You know most people think I'm crazy, right? I'm the chaotic one in their orderly world. But, I think most people are chaotically uninteresting. Be *interesting* with me, Kyle," she said, hugging him around his neck.

Kyle didn't know what to say. He'd never met anyone like her, and he hated the thought of saying "goodbye." What could he do except offer her the one thing he had to give? "I need to tell you something."

"Anything," she said.

"Allaire, I can't believe I'm saying this, but I want to take this leap with you. If there was a way, I'd be in . . . But there's not . . . I'm . . . This is gonna sound absolutely crazy, but somehow I think you're going to believe me. I've come here from the year 2016."

"Wow," she said. "Maybe we really can live in Crazy Town together."

"I'm serious," he said. "I know it's nuts. But, I went through this thing . . . "

"Uh, okay, *future man*," she said, leaning against his shoulder. "Where's your time machine?"

Kyle put his hand into his pocket and pulled out the silk blot, which had shrunk to the size of a coaster. "I came through this."

Allaire poked at the silk blot with her finger. "Feels like a piece of fabric."

Kyle shrugged. "It's fine if you don't believe me. I don't know if I would. But this thing leads to a metal tunnel, with exits marked for every different year. I'm here to stop something horrible from happening. I really can't tell you any more than that. But that's the reason that all of this . . . we just can't."

Allaire sat studying his face for a few seconds. "Okay, I'll buy it. I *do* believe you."

"Just like that?" Kyle asked.

"Just like that," she answered. "But, I don't care *when* you come from. You're here now. That's what matters." She grabbed his face and kissed him, using her weight to push him to the ground. He couldn't believe how unaffected she was by what he'd told her. "And, you know what kind of person travels through time to try to fix the future? An awesome one!"

Kyle pulled away from the kiss. "You don't get it. I have to get back into the tunnel tomorrow afternoon or I'm stuck here forever, which means at some point, I may run into the younger version of myself and my head will explode. Not to mention the fact that, according to the lady who sent me here, the timestream doesn't want me here and is going to do whatever it takes to get me out." The words sounded crazy. He couldn't believe how much things had changed for him in only a few days.

"I don't care about tomorrow," she said. "In the

morning, say "goodbye" if you need to. But, give me tonight."

She climbed on top of him once more, wrapping her legs around his and pushing against his body with hers. This time, Kyle had no interest in stopping her, so he didn't.

CHAPTER 13

KYLE OPENED HIS EYES AND SQUINTED IN THE morning sunlight. After they'd made love, Kyle had told Allaire absolutely everything: the crash, the prison, his father. Then they spent the night pressed against each other in her sleeping bag.

Panic set in almost immediately when he realized that he only had until about seven o'clock this evening to convince his father to stop the accident sixteen years from now, return to New York City and get back into the silk blot. He was surprised to find himself alone in the field behind Silverman High. He brought his arm in front of him and craned his head to find "BE RIGHT BACK" written in the same dark red color as Allaire's lips.

He rubbed the sleepiness from his eyes and stood up. Just as he finished peeing in the bushes lining the school, he saw a couple of buses pull up down the street. Pretty soon, the area would be teeming with students from Silverman High—kids nearly his age, but ones who hadn't made such huge, life-altering mistakes. He turned around and saw Allaire walking toward him holding a bag and couple of cups.

"You a cream and sugar guy?" she asked with her flirty smile. "I guessed black, but I brought some fixings you could add."

"Black is fine," Kyle said, taking one of the coffees. The prison's instant packets were gross enough to dissuade Kyle from a daily caffeine habit at Stevenson Youth.

Allaire sat on the ground and opened the bag, pulling out two clear containers with scrambled eggs and potatoes in them. She handed one to

Kyle. "Big day for you, future man. What's our plan?"

Kyle opened up his container of eggs and pulled one of the cheap plastic forks from the bag. He started on the eggs like he hadn't eaten in days, which wasn't too far from the truth. "Last night was the best night I've had for as long as I can remember."

"Same time, same place tonight, then?" Allaire asked, winking at him. "After you go and save the children, of course."

"I can't tell if you actually believe me or not," Kyle said, smiling at her.

"Oh, I believe you," she said, turning her voice a shade more to the serious side.

"Y'know, I think you're pretty perfect," Kyle said. If he'd met her in a world he belonged in, Kyle could see entering one of those relationship vortexes with her. One of those long honeymoon periods where March became July and neither person ever even realized they'd lost track of time.

"I don't want you to go back," she said, grabbing his hand. "You don't have to."

Kyle put his hand on her leg and squeezed her thigh. "I have a job to do. If I don't, kids are going to die."

"Do what you need to do and come back to me," she said. "Why do you need to go back to 2016?"

"We have to get you back on the bus to the city," Kyle said.

"We could go live somewhere else," she said. "Away from Flemming. Away from anywhere you'd ever see yourself. You know how many people there are in the world? And neither of us have seen any of it!"

Kyle shook his head. He was scared that betraying Myrna would spell doom for the kids on the bus. "You're the second once-in-a-lifetime thing that's happened to me this week. I'm sorry, Allaire. I have to go back tonight. And if you don't get on that bus right now, I'm afraid I won't do what I need to to save those kids."

Allaire wiped her eyes, and nodded. Then, like she was convincing herself of something, she nodded over and over again. Kyle hated the hurt he saw in her face.

Allaire sobbed, and then took a deep breath. She stabbed the plastic fork into her breakfast container.

"Eggs are *that* good, huh?" Kyle asked, hoping he might get her to crack a smile. He lifted her chin with his hand. "I hate that we have to say goodbye—"

"Then don't," she said.

"I wasn't even supposed to speak to anyone except my father," Kyle said.

"Well don't worry. Your secrets are safe with me, Kyle Cash," she said with more of a polite smile than the loving one he was becoming addicted to. She stood up.

"Let me walk you to the station," he said.

"You don't need to," Allaire said. "Do your thing. I'll go home now. I promise."

Kyle nodded slowly. He wanted every last second with her, but he had a long road ahead of him today and needed every second he had.

She kissed him, long and deep as the night before. "Promise me one thing," she said.

"What?"

"That you'll come find me in 2016."

He put his hands on her cheeks. "You'll be twice my age, Allaire. You'll probably be married. Maybe you'll have kids."

"No!" she said. "Don't say that. You have to promise me. Or I'm not getting on that bus."

"You're not even going to remember me," Kyle said.

"That's insulting," she said, shaking her head in disappointment. "I've never felt this way before, Kyle."

Kyle put his hands on her shoulders. "I'm sorry. I just—"

She still looked disappointed. "You're not even the one that has to wait." Kyle felt like he had somehow minimized what had happened between them by presenting the idea of a world where she moved on from him at some point in the next eighteen years.

"I'm really sorry," he said.

"Don't be. Just come find me," she said. "And make sure to tell me I'm still pretty."

"Of course you'll still be pretty," he said, hugging her now. "You'll still be beautiful."

"I'll be thirty-four!" she said. "That's old!"

"I have to go," he said, squeezing her once more.

"Good luck, Kyle Cash," she said, as he began to walk away. Immediately, he started to think about what he was going to say to his father.

"Thank you," Allaire called after him.

Kyle turned around. "Thank you?"

"For letting me love you for these two days," she answered.

He had no doubt she meant it, but his mind was already someplace else. "Thank you too," he said, and then he was off.

CHAPTER 14

IT TOOK KYLE A FEW PASSES THROUGH THE underground parking garage of Crespi Memorial Hospital before he found the white Nissan Sentra. Still new, and still Sillow's car, it looked like a different vehicle to him. All of the bumps and bruises the car had picked up in the time Kyle and his mom had driven it into the ground were gone. Or, more accurately, they weren't there yet. And it was so much cleaner than Kyle could ever manage to get it, even after a car wash.

Kyle had broken into the car once before, but he'd needed a wire hanger. He smiled when he saw, though, that the passenger window had been left open just a little bit. He squished his arm inside and felt his hairs ripping out as he reached for the button on the inside of the door. He flicked it up, pulled his arm out quickly, and opened the door of the car.

Moments later, Kyle stood at the information booth on the main floor of the hospital. "How can I help you?" the bored looking woman on duty asked him.

"I was on my way to the elevator when I saw a car in one of the hospital employee spaces with its lights on," Kyle said.

"Oh?" she said.

"White Nissan Sentra," he said. "Looks like it's probably a '96?"

"What a nice boy you are," she said, smiling. "I'll make an announcement."

Back underground, Kyle hustled to his father's car and was about to duck inside when he saw someone running through the parking lot toward him. It was a woman wearing a black baseball cap—the same blond woman who had witnessed Ochoa's head exploding. She ran away last time before Kyle could get a better look, but he was positive this was her.

Kyle took a step back from the car when he noticed that she was carrying a gun as she ran full speed toward him.

Behind him, Kyle heard a metal door slam loudly. He turned the other way and saw Allaire walking toward him, smiling bashfully. "I know, I know, I wasn't supposed—"

"Allaire, get down," he yelled.

He turned around again and saw the blond woman with the cap stop dead in her tracks, almost skidding forward from the sudden change of course. With a look of panic on her face, she turned and ran the other way just as fast as she'd come toward him. Within a few seconds, she'd turned a corner and was out of view.

When Kyle turned again, Allaire was standing right next to him.

"What was that all about?" he wondered out loud.

"I know I was supposed to go back," Allaire said.

"Allaire, you shouldn't be here," Kyle said. His father would be down there any minute. "It's not safe."

She pulled a CD out of her jacket and shoved it in his direction. "Here. It's a present for you. I made it at the record store yesterday. It's a mix."

Kyle took it. "Thank you," he said, smiling at her, hoping she would just turn and go.

"They're all my favorite songs," she said, loosening her posture. "I'm sure they're oldies where you're from. I'm guessing Hanson is a one-hit wonder, but Third-Eye Blind seems like they have staying power."

"You really need to go right now," he said.

She rose to her tiptoes to give him a kiss on the cheek and then turned away slowly without saying anything. Kyle followed her to the exit with his eyes, waiting to make sure she left.

He glanced the other way, and there was no sign of the blond woman anymore. She'd changed course abruptly and gotten herself away from him as quickly as she could. He wondered who she was, whether she knew his secret, and why she'd freaked out and left. It was too much of a coincidence that she'd shown up twice now.

Sillow opened the driver's side door of the Sentra and bent inside the car enough to reach for the lights.

Kyle popped up from behind the driver's seat and grabbed him by the collar of his hospital scrubs, pulling him into the car. "Close the door,"

Kyle said as he stuck the Revolutionary War era pistol through the space between the seat and the headrest, pointing it against the back of Sillow's neck. Since he had no ammo for the centuries-old weapon, concealing it from his view was the only hope Kyle had of convincing Sillow he was armed.

Sillow slammed the door shut. "You again, huh? Every single time I've owed, I've paid. Why's he got his panties in a knot so bad this time?"

"This isn't about money," Kyle answered, trying to sound tougher and older than he was.

"Bullshit," Sillow said. "It's *always* about money."

"Not this time," Kyle said. "I have no idea what you owe, or who you owe it to."

"Then what the fuck are you doin' in my car?" Sillow asked. "With a fuckin' gun to my head?"

Kyle opened the rear, driver's side door. "Don't move." He stepped out of the car and walked around to enter the car from the passenger side. He tried to conceal the pistol as he lowered himself into the passenger seat by holding his jacket in front of it.

Sillow leaned back in the seat, peeking at the gun. "What do you have there?"

"A gun," Kyle answered. His pulse quickened even more. "Don't move."

Sillow lifted his right hand and hung it in the air. "You mean like this?" The moment Kyle turned his head, Sillow grabbed at the pistol under Kyle's jacket with his left hand, clutching it by its barrel. Kyle squeezed it, desperate to hold on. "What the . . . ?" Sillow jerked his hand away and pulled the gun away from Kyle.

"How old is this thing?" Sillow asked with a wicked smile. "Ain't even loaded." He tossed the gun onto the floor of the backseat. He grabbed Kyle by the throat, choking him against the headrest.

Kyle grabbed Sillow's hands and tried to pry them off of his neck. "I need to talk to you." He had no idea what to say next. He had about as much in common with his father as he did with the steering wheel.

"Get talkin' then. You prob'ly got thirty seconds 'til you pass out," Sillow said.

He was desperate to get Sillow off of his throat. Instead, Sillow pushed harder and Kyle felt his breakfast coming up as he struggled to breathe. Kyle grabbed for the door handle and pulled it, but the door was locked. "I need you to do something for me."

"Is that so?" Sillow asked, grinning.

"It's important. It's going to save people's lives . . . Kids' lives," Kyle said, beginning to lose hope that he had the right words at his disposal to stop Sillow from choking him out.

"What kids?" Sillow asked, loosening his grip just a bit. He looked interested now, which surprised Kyle.

"There's a chance to save twelve kids," Kyle said. "There's a bus crash that happens in—"

"Mutherfucker," Sillow said, pulling his hands

away, looking through the windows of the car now. "You're Kyle."

Kyle nodded. "I'm your son."

Sillow gave him an amused smile. "What are you, sixteen? Seventeen?"

"Eighteen," Kyle answered. "How did you—?"

Sillow got out of the car, still carrying an amused look, and Kyle followed. Sillow's face softened as he spoke over the car. "I'm sorry about chokin' you. What'd you expect? My son! How 'bout that?"

Kyle wouldn't be born for another month here in 1998. He looked at the clock inside Sillow's car: 11:32 AM.

Maybe Sillow was capable of stopping the crash after all. Perhaps he could follow through on what Kyle needed from him sixteen years from now. "I haven't got much time," Kyle said.

"You come to tell me the same thing the other guy did?" Sillow asked. "Before he got shot up."

"What other guy?" Kyle asked.

Sillow cocked his eyebrow disbelievingly. "The other guy. From the future."

Kyle stood there completely stunned.

Sillow started walking toward the garage exit.

"Where are you going?" Kyle asked him.

"I guess I'll let you buy me that steak now," Sillow said. "Son!"

CHAPTER 15

"WHO'S THIS OTHER PERSON?" KYLE ASKED AS they walked toward the restaurant. "What did he look like?"

Sillow looked Kyle in the eyes. "You ain't gonna get shot like him, are you? I was damn near hit, too."

Kyle thought of the blond woman. "I hope not."

Already today Kyle had spent more time with his father than he'd spent since the first year of his life. He couldn't imagine how his mother would've chosen this man to have a baby with, but at least he wasn't hitting him or choking him out now.

"Damn lunch menu," Sillow said, after sitting

down in the sticky, upholstered booth. "I'm askin' if they can do the Ribeye, even though it ain't on the menu. And I'm gettin' the salad bar too. I like the macaroni salad."

Sillow looked at Kyle, as if he might object. Like Kyle, by virtue of having a few dollars in his pocket, was the parent.

The waitress came by and took Sillow's order. When she left, he just stared out the window.

"Where do I live in 2014?" Sillow asked with a conspiratorial smile. "Tell me somethin', at least . . . Like, who wins the Super Bowl next year?"

Now, Kyle was quiet. His whole life he'd wanted to confront his dad, to ask him why he'd been such a shitty father. He'd run through the conversation more times than he could count. Yet now, sitting here across from the man, Kyle couldn't say any of it without risking changes to the future with consequences he couldn't imagine.

He couldn't tell Sillow what it was like to have your mom take you to see The Rock when WWE came to town. Or how desperate Kyle was to please every authority figure he'd ever met, just hoping their approval might fill in a part of him that not having a father had left empty.

Even crazier was that *this* Sillow—still in his mid-20s, still in love with Kyle's mother—hadn't done wrong by him yet. Kyle knew there might be some combination of words that could change their entire lives, and give him a father to grow up with. Or at least one who didn't completely abandon him.

"Believe me, I wish I could, but I really can't tell you anything more than you need to know," Kyle said. "You said someone else came to see you. Who was it?"

Sillow looked lost in thought for a moment, his eyes fixed on the parking lot. He didn't know anything definitively about the next eighteen years, but Kyle wondered if he had an idea already that he wasn't cut out for parenthood. Then, with a quick nod, he looked Kyle in the eyes. "Alright," he said.

"What do you want to know? Uh . . . The other guy . . . It was a long time ago—maybe seven, eight years . . . "

"What did he tell you?"

"He couldn't really *tell* me anything. I get a knock on my door. I was home by myself at the time. I open the door, and this guy, he's standing there. He was in bad shape . . . I mean, he was actually in good shape, but looked like he was gonna pass out—like he'd been running for hours. Just dripping with sweat. Wearing a suit too! A black one. Couldn't catch his breath . . . Maybe a little older than you, but not much past his twenties. Whole suit was completely soaked through—I don't know whether it was sweat, or water, or what."

"Go on," Kyle said.

"He starts talkin' to me," Sillow said. "But it sounds more like a whisper, but with water in it. Like a . . . gurgle. He says 'you need to stop the bust crash,' and I say 'bust crash?' And he shakes his head 'no.'"

"Bus crash," Kyle said.

"I guess so," Sillow answered. "Never got to hear him say anything else, except, 'Don't let your son Kyle in the car.' And then he said 'March 13, 2014.'"

Kyle hung on every word. *Who was this person? Who'd sent him back?* He wondered. "What else did he say?"

"Nothing," Sillow answered. "Got his damn head blown off. Someone must've had a sniper rifle in the building across the street from me—that's what the police thought, at least. Blew his head clear off with the first shot. Hit the door frame to my apartment with the second shot."

"How'd he know about the accident?" Kyle wondered aloud.

"How would I know? I got the fuck out of dodge after that shit," Sillow said. "Went and stayed at my buddy Ricky's for a month. Cooperated with the police mostly. I didn't tell them what the guy said to me, because I was never sure I heard him right. Also didn't want to sound fuckin' crazy. I don't think they ever ID'd the body neither."

Kyle looked down nervously. "Were you, I mean, are you planning on doing what he asked you to do?"

"In, what, 2014?" Sillow asked. "I don't know. I mean, I wrote the date down. I remember it. But, I don't have a kid . . . Not yet, at least . . . Shit, you know you look nothin' like me, right?"

Kyle considered this new piece of information. If someone had already traveled back and the crash had still happened, maybe whatever Sillow was going to do in 2014 wasn't going to be enough to make a difference.

"If you were going to do what the man asked, how do you think you'd try to stop me from getting into the car?" Kyle asked. "You'd probably take my keys—"

Sillow shrugged. "I don't know. Maybe."

"Maybe you need to do more than that?" Kyle

asked, really thinking out loud more than asking for Sillow's input.

"Uh, sure, okay," Sillow said.

"I think the reason I'm here," Kyle said, "is because when the other guy came to see you, I don't think he convinced you to do it."

"To be honest, man, I didn't really give it that much thought. It was weird, but I didn't know what else to think," Sillow said. "I do think about that bullet that nearly killed me comin' through the window, though."

The waitress laid a huge steak in front of Sillow and he immediately started cutting a bite.

Kyle nodded. This entire thing. Myrna. The trip through time. The fact that it had to be his father. It was all starting to make sense. "That's the whole point. You didn't think much about it," Kyle said. "I get it now. That guy in the suit failed!"

"He got his head blown straight off," Sillow said. "I'd say he failed."

"I flipped Joe's car and killed those kids anyway,

so someone figured out that they had to send me back to see you . . . "

"Who's Joe?" Sillow asked, and Kyle got a chill. *Joe!* As Sillow sliced into his steak, Kyle played the morning of the crash over in his head. Having a photographic memory meant that every time Kyle relived that day, it was in vivid detail. Everything from what he ate for breakfast, to what he and Joe talked about while they smoked and drank. It was all there. Except for one piece, which was foggy to Kyle. He remembered seeing his tires were slashed, but it wasn't nearly as vivid as the hundreds of thousands of other memories he'd stored up about that day and replayed over and over to himself. Same with going to Joe's house and driving his car to school. The moments in his head before the crash were vivid, but those moments leading right up to it were not. He knew that his tires had been slashed, but he had a lot of trouble picturing them, which was very unusual for him.

"Oh my God," Kyle said. "Wait a second . . .

You *did* it! You *were* there. It was you that morning! You slashed my tires. You're the one my mom heard when she stopped back home!" Kyle imagined Sillow that morning, hiding somewhere in the backyard so Kyle or his mother wouldn't spot him.

"Uh, okay," Sillow answered. "So I *did* do . . . or, I'm gonna do, what the guy told me to?"

"You *did!*," Kyle said. "But, we had another way to get to school. We took my friend Joe's car, and that just replaced my car in the bus crash. Slashing my tires wasn't enough to keep me from being in the same place."

"So, why didn't someone tell me I needed to slash those tires too?" Sillow asked while chewing a huge bite of steak.

Kyle's mind raced. *Was there a version of the bus crash that had taken place in his Sentra?* It was unusual that they'd take Joe's fancier car to school, so that would make sense. At least as much as *anything* could make sense in a world where it was possible to travel through time, and live the same moment more than once.

"I think you did what you were supposed to do. You didn't let me get into *my* car," Kyle said. "I think you did change the future. You did it! We just had another option. We took Joe's car."

Kyle was sure of it, the more he thought it through: in 2014 as Kyle had lived through it, Sillow did what the man in the black suit asked of him. He came to New York and slashed Kyle's tires. He just hadn't done enough to stop the accident from happening, because the boys were able to walk to Joe's house and drive his Audi to school. Myrna had told Kyle that time resists change. *And if something resists,* Kyle thought to himself, *then you need to push harder.*

If Kyle's theory was right, he hoped there was something more that Sillow could do to make sure the entire accident never happened in the first place.

"So, what now?" Sillow asked. "I slash your

friend's tires too? Everybody lives happily ever after?"

Kyle shook his head. "I don't think it's gonna be that simple."

"And there's no one else who can do this for you?" Sillow asked. "I, uh . . . This is a lot of responsibility to lay on a guy."

"No," Kyle said. "You're my father. I need *you* to help me."

"You know, this is some complicated shit," Sillow said, shoving a forkful of steak and potato into his mouth. "And, it ain't *my* complicated shit neither."

"You're involved already," Kyle said. "I can't tell you everything that happens in your life after I leave here today . . . But what I will tell you is this: Everyone has regrets. Some people have more than others. Whatever yours are, come March 13, 2014, if you do this for me, the slate's clean. You will have done the one thing I ever asked of you, and all accounts are settled as far as we're concerned."

"You make it sound like I'm gonna have a lot to make up for," Sillow said. "To be honest, I ain't surprised. I didn't know my parents, so what the fuck would I know about being one?"

"I'm here to change one thing on one day," Kyle said. "So just, do whatever . . . Guilt free, even. Just make sure you come through on March 13, 2014." He couldn't believe he was actually encouraging his father to become the deadbeat he'd always been.

"Alright. Okay. So, I just gotta find a way to keep you in your house, right?" Sillow asked. "You don't leave, you can't cause a crash."

Kyle hit the table with his hands. "What if school gets cancelled somehow?"

"Like, I flood the school, or call in a bomb threat or somethin'?" Sillow asked.

Kyle looked at a calendar hanging behind Sizzler's cash register. Sillow wasn't privy to the last eighteen years of news events like Kyle was. "Not a bomb threat," he said, thinking about Columbine and 9/11. He certainly didn't want to create a version of the future where his father was in jail.

"There's another way," Kyle said.

As he started to lay out the plan, Kyle was heartened to see his father actually listening. Sillow even wrote a few things down on a Sizzler placemat. After all, it would be almost two decades before he had to implement the plan. It wasn't foolproof by any stretch, and dangerous too. But an okay plan was better than none. Kyle just hoped no one else would get killed in the process of carrying it out.

They finished the meal without much chitchat beyond strategizing for Sillow's success sixteen years in the future.

A little later, as he watched his father walk away from Sizzler, back toward Crespi Memorial Hospital, Kyle felt a lump in his throat.

Kyle had accidentally wound up in the system after a horrible mistake, while Sillow, if he wasn't living his life outside of the margins of the law, certainly seemed to enjoy being on the wrong side of good taste. Whatever Kyle's mother saw in him at the time, Kyle wasn't surprised that the relationship didn't last. Watching his father go to town on that steak had been the first time they'd ever shared a meal. And, it was likely the last as well. They parted with a handshake and before he even let go, he regretted being too shy to hug his father for the first time in his life.

CHAPTER 16

KYLE ARRIVED BACK AT THE PORT AUTHORITY Bus Terminal in New York City just before seven o'clock. He had about fifteen minutes to get back to the construction site where they were building Stevenson Youth Correctional, and up to the unfinished third floor. Hopefully, then, the silk blot would open for him again and he could return to 2016.

The question that kept playing in Kyle's head again and again was whether he felt he really needed to return at all . . .

He looked in the direction of the uptown A/C/E train line. He hated that he'd left Allaire crying. If he went back through the time tunnel, the chance of ever being with her again was remote. But, Kyle kept coming to what he'd seen happen to Ochoa. There was no way to guarantee he wouldn't, at some point, come face to face with his younger self. He looked from the subway platform to the exit up to the street. Back and forth. Over and over. He reached into his pocket for the Metrocard Allaire had let him keep. For a brief moment, he decided he would go see her and miss his window to go back. But, the card wasn't in his pocket. Gone. He remembered Myrna telling him that the timestream would want him out of 1998. Or, he could've just dropped it somewhere. He considered jumping the turnstile, but an announcement stopped him. He strained to hear it through the static of the old speaker.

"Uptown A, C and E trains are going out of service for track maintenance. We apologize for the delay. Please use the shuttle bus located upstairs at . . ."

"What the hell?" Kyle heard from behind him. It was an older man complaining to the token booth clerk. "A freakin' shuttle bus?" Kyle turned and headed for the exit up to the street.

It was drizzling when Kyle got to the construction site a couple of minutes before seven o'clock. He was cutting it close, and couldn't afford another delay now that he'd decided on going back to 2016. It was quiet, but a few guys probably pulling overtime still occupied the future location of Stevenson Youth Correctional. He kicked the chain link fence around the site lightly until he found a spot where he might be able to lift it and push himself through. He ducked down into the weeds, nearly stepping in a pile of dog shit as he did.

He shimmied through the small opening on his stomach, until he was at the edge of the site. Most of the dozers, lifts and excavators sat empty, waiting for tomorrow. Kyle looked around to make sure no one was looking his way and then moved as quickly as he could to the corner of the unfinished building. He'd have to get up two of the tall metal ladders on the building's skeleton to reach the third floor. He remembered from their way down that each ladder had eighteen rungs.

"Hey!" a voice called out, as Kyle started to climb. "Hey, guy. You can't be in here . . . What . . . ? What're you doin'?"

Kyle started climbing as fast as he could when he saw two construction workers running toward him. One of them was on his walkie-talkie, probably calling the police. There was no benefit to stopping when Kyle had only about six minutes to spare.

He started onto the second ladder. He tried to move fast, but his foot slipped on the slick metal. He hung by his arms for a second, barely escaping a fall. He looked down as the two guys underneath gained on him. They negotiated the ladder much more easily than Kyle did.

Before he could reach the third floor, Kyle looked down and saw he was only a few rungs ahead of a mountainous construction worker. Kyle tried to move quickly, but the construction worker managed to grab Kyle's right ankle, stopping his progress completely. Kyle lifted his right knee up, trying to pull his foot away, but he had no luck pulling away from the ox who used his strong hands to keep his grip. Kyle looked down and noticed that the man's nails had left a bloody scratch on his leg. He tried kicking at the man's left hand clinging to the ladder, but couldn't connect.

Kyle pulled one hand off the ladder, and grabbed the silk blot from his pocket. He wasn't in exactly the same place that he and Ochoa had come through on their way out of the silk blot, but if he didn't give it a shot now, he might never get the chance.

He looked down at the huge construction guy,

who squinted his eyes at the strange piece of fabric in Kyle's hand. "What the hell?" the guy asked him, loosening his grip on Kyle's foot just a bit.

Kyle curled his left arm around the back of the ladder, basically hanging by the crease of his elbow. He looked down and tried pulling his foot away again, but no luck. He held the silk blot in both hands and pulled it over his head like a shirt. All of a sudden, his head was completely engulfed in darkness. He no longer felt the pull of the construction worker on his leg, and easily pulled the rest of his body into the silk blot. Once inside, he used the dim light emanating from the silk blot to look at the cut on his leg which was bothering him. He saw that the construction worker's nails had made a deep gash, but Kyle could barely believe his eyes as he watched the cut heal within a few seconds. It was unlike anything he'd seen before. Like watching a time-lapse video.

Even though he'd just spent two days in the past, so much about 'time weaving' was still a mystery to Kyle. He wondered what it was about the tunnel that could heal a wound so quickly. And strangely, he had even discovered that one of the 'rules' told to him—that he'd need to exit and enter the silk blot in the same place—didn't seem to be exactly true.

He'd be back in 2016 in a few hours, and would find out if Sillow had come through for him. Or, if he'd failed, which would mean that Ochoa died for nothing.

And if Sillow had been successful, Kyle—not an inmate any longer—would have to explain to the prison's guards how he managed to break *into* one of the cells in their prison.

CHAPTER 17

KYLE WATCHED FROM THE BATHROOM WINDOW as his mom got back into her car and headed off. If she'd come upstairs, he and Joe would have been caught, no question. His mom probably suspected he smoked weed, but had no idea how often, and certainly not inside of her house.

Kyle sprayed enough Lysol in the small bathroom to choke a small animal, and he opened the window. He gave another look at the ridiculous wallpaper with the green elephants balancing huge serving platters, and smiled. He'd always liked the design better when he was high.

"Where'd I leave my phone?" Joe asked.

"In the basement next to mine," Kyle said. "Yours is on the right side of the table lamp. Mine's on the left."

"Freak," Joe answered. Kyle's crazy memory still shocked the people in his life, no matter how often he put it on display.

Kyle opened the bathroom door and headed out into the hallway. He grabbed the bannister and was about to head downstairs when he heard the screen door at the back of the house squeak open, and then slam shut. He heard footsteps. "Shit," he whispered. "She's back." He put a finger over his lips, signaling Joe to be quiet, and grabbed the front of Joe's jacket pulling him back into the bathroom. Kyle closed the bathroom door quickly and quietly.

"I didn't even hear her car, dude," Joe said, more loudly than Kyle hoped.

Kyle tiptoed into the shower again and looked out the window. "What the fuck?" he said, his heart beating faster as adrenaline pumped through him. "Her car's not there."

"Who the hell is in your house then?" Joe asked.

Kyle heard footsteps coming up the stairs now. "Shit. This is not good. Shit. Shit. Shit." Kyle knew this wasn't just weed paranoia. Someone was in his house, and he didn't think it was his mother.

"Maybe your mom parked in front of the house?" Joe said.

"Shhhhh!"

The footsteps continued to the top of the stairs, and stopped outside the bathroom door.

"Should we open it?" Joe whispered.

"Are you crazy?" Kyle whispered back. "No way."

He watched the knob of the door move. He held his breath. But, the knob didn't turn, it just shifted a little. He heard a click. Then, the footsteps headed away from the door and back downstairs.

Kyle tried the knob, but it wouldn't turn.

"Someone just locked us in," Kyle whispered. "Whoever the hell that is just locked us in here!"

"Why the hell do you have a lock on the outside of the door?" Joe asked.

Kyle shrugged. "Old house? I don't know." he whispered. "Why am I even whispering?" Kyle stood with his face to the door now, and pounded on it with his fist. "Hello!!"

He put his ear to the door. Whoever it was was still in the house, walking around downstairs. "You think we're getting robbed?" Kyle asked Joe.

"It's gonna suck if they take our phones, dude," Joe answered.

Sillow still felt rattled from his flight into New York the night before. He looked around his ex-wife's living room trying to find a remote control. He was curious about whether his plane's crash landing would be on the news. He would stay here for a couple of hours like Kyle told him to, back in 1998, making sure the boys didn't leave that upstairs bathroom. Then, later, he'd unlock the door and try to get out without being seen. He hadn't thought much about the house in years. He and Stella were so happy to inherit it from her father when he died. Sillow never imagined he'd be back here after he left.

The house looked almost identical to the way it did the day he bailed. He wondered if Stella still had that stupid elephant wallpaper in the upstairs bathroom. Even the ugly green couch must've been going on two decades now. Not that he was living like royalty either, he thought to himself. He, Raquel and the twins got by in Florida, but it was nothing fancy. And he was missing a day and a half of work to be here, which would make things tighter this month. Sillow had considered cancelling his ticket up until he passed the deadline to get a refund, but he'd promised to square the tab with his kid, and somehow this felt big enough to really make up for at least some of his mistakes.

Sillow found the remote and turned on channel 4, sitting down on the familiar green couch. Sinking into it, he understood why you wouldn't just give it up.

As he scanned through stations, looking for coverage of his crazy landing, he heard a squeak at the back door. Suddenly the door swung open, and a woman in a black hat moved inside quickly. As she turned coming through the door, he noticed the unmistakable bulge of a gun stuck in the waist of her pants. She held a combat knife which looked like a set of brass knuckles with a curved blade attached to them. The woman moved toward Sillow, stopping a few feet away. "You have three seconds . . . Where is he?" She spoke like she was racing to get the words out of her mouth.

Sillow put his hands in front of him, trying to calm her and signal that he had no interest in a fight. "Hey lady, hold on. I don't think you understand what's going on here. There are, uh, lives at stake here!"

She walked forward and pushed the blade against Sillow's throat. "Right now, the only life you should be concerned with saving is your own. Where is Kyle?"

Kyle heard the screen door downstairs screech closed again. "There's two of them down there," Kyle said. "I hear them talking."

Joe looked less fazed than he probably should, given the situation. He pulled the blunt out of his coat pocket.

"Not now! What the hell are you thinking?" Kyle snapped, grabbing the blunt from Joe and putting it in his pocket. "How the hell did they know we were in here?"

Kyle felt a sense of dread and started making promises with God, even though he'd never felt sure about exactly what he believed. *If we get out of this,* he thought to himself, *I won't take my good grades—or my mother—for granted. I'll stop getting high every morning. I'll be the good kid my mom thinks I am.*

"Who are you?" Sillow asked the woman.

"Is he upstairs?" she asked.

When Sillow didn't say anything, she pressed the blade against his throat. "It doesn't matter who I am. What matters is getting Kyle on his way to school."

"You know, don't you?" Sillow asked. *Had Kyle told her about the accident too?* "You know what's gonna go down today if he leaves this house."

"It has to happen," the woman answered.

Something clunked above them and they both looked toward the stairs.

The blond woman walked quickly to the stairs

and started up, two at a time. Sillow hadn't anticipated putting himself in harm's way to help the son he had no relationship with. He was already inconveniencing himself. Sillow watched her head upstairs, the blade in her hand, and took a deep breath before getting up and following her. Sneaking up behind her, he lunged toward her left leg, and hung on it, trying to pull her to the ground.

But the blond woman grabbed the bannister for balance and raised her legs, delivering a hard drop kick to Sillow's chest. He tumbled down the steps to the landing at the bottom. She followed him down.

"Those kids on the bus are gonna die," Sillow said, looking up at her. "Why not at least try to stop it?"

She pulled her right leg back now, and delivered a crushing kick underneath his chin with her black Dr. Marten boot. The kick caught Sillow in the soft area between his chin and his Adam's apple. He gagged and felt like he might throw up.

She bounded up the stairs toward the bathroom.

"Don't hurt Kyle," Sillow tried to call out as he held his throat and tried to catch his breath.

***

Bruno nervously fiddled with the keys to the school bus as he took the last sip of the espresso his wife Lucilla made for him. He had to leave soon to pick up the kids for morning dropoff at Clinton Middle School, but wanted to see the next story on the Today Show.

"You see this thing that happened last night?" he asked. "Plane's gears for landing didn't come down. They're about to show a video on the television."

"Were the people hurt?" Lucilla asked.

"No, thank Christ," Bruno answered.

"You really need to get to work," she said.

"Please!" Bruno said, a little more harshly than he preferred to be with her. "I just want to see this thing on the news. It's five more minutes." She'd been encouraging him to give up the bus route for years. She was right when she pointed out that the kids tried his patience, but he felt like being around them kept him young. And he liked to get out of the house for a couple of hours in the mornings and the afternoons.

The Today Show came back, leading with a video of the Western Airlines plane skidding into the runway, sparks flying, wobbling and bouncing until it came to a jarring stop. Bruno's stomach churned thinking about their son Francesco who flew all over the place for work.

"You know how many planes land every day with no problems?" Lucilla asked. "Now, go. Those kids need to get to school, *mi amore.*" He looked at his watch and hurried out to the bus. He was fifteen minutes late for morning pickups.

"What the hell are they doing down there?" Kyle asked Joe. "It sounds like they're wrestling."

"Maybe the cops came, and they're arresting whoever broke in," Joe said.

Kyle took the blunt from his pocket and tossed it into the toilet. "Then maybe we don't need to have this in here right now."

"Dick," Joe said.

There was a knock at the bathroom door.

"Who's there?" Kyle answered, his heart thumping as hard as it ever had.

"I'm going to get you out of there," a female voice said, "but you need to listen to me carefully."

Kyle exchanged a look with Joe, who finally looked as freaked out as Kyle felt. "Who's there?" Kyle asked.

"It doesn't matter," the voice said. "Everything's fine. You just need to go to school and have a normal day. If you do that, everything's going to be fine."

"Are you the police?" Kyle asked.

"Yes," she said. "We had a report of an intrusion, and it's been taken care of. I need you to get to school now so I don't have to cite you for truancy."

"No!" a man's voice shouted. "It's not what she says. Don't—" The voice stopped suddenly as Kyle heard a loud pop. He'd never heard one before, but Kyle thought it might be a gun shot.

Now, he was in a full-on panic, his stomach fluttering with fear. Joe crouched down in the bathtub, and Kyle squeezed himself between the toilet and the sink, trying to use the porcelain of the toilet to block him from anything—like a bullet—that might come through the door.

"I'm going to unlock this door. What I need you to do," the female voice continued, "is to stay in there for a few minutes. I want you to count to two hundred before you come out. Count slowly, okay? And loud enough so I can hear you."

Kyle nodded, as if she could see him. "One . . . Two . . . Three . . ."

With the gun pressed against the back of his head, Sillow had no choice but to climb into the trunk as she instructed. As he climbed inside, he noticed the tire jack he'd bought for the Sentra almost twenty years ago was still in there.

"I hear one kick, one scream, one *anything*, then you can be sure the next shot I take won't miss," the blond woman said.

Sillow laid down to get his head out of the way, and watched the trunk of the Sentra slam shut over him.

From the moment Kyle opened the bathroom door, the boys sprinted until they were through the house and out to the driveway. Kyle looked all around him for some evidence of what had just happened. Outside at least, there was nothing out of place.

"Can we get the fuck out of here?" Joe asked.

"We should call the police," Kyle said.

Joe wrinkled his brow. "Are you fucking crazy?" he asked. "We're fucking hammered."

"I'm not *hammered*," Kyle said. Joe had definitely hit more of the tequila than he had. "Then let's go to school, at least."

Kyle started toward his car, but noticed the flats immediately. "Look," he said, pointing the tires out to Joe. "Shit."

"Let's go to my house" Joe said, starting down the driveway toward the street.

Kyle looked at his watch. He'd forgotten about Meltzner's math quiz while they were locked in the bathroom, and now there was no chance he'd make it before nine. Maybe his excuse would be good enough to satisfy his teacher. "Let's take your car to school," Kyle said.

Joe started walking out of the driveway, toward

his house. "I'm too fucked up to drive," he said. "Let's go chill at my house for a bit, and then we'll go to school later."

"Do me a favor, Joe? Today's been fucked up enough. If you don't want to call the police, can we please just go to school? We know we'll be safe there. I'll drive your car if you want. Please?" Kyle asked.

Joe looked at Kyle and rolled his eyes. "Whatever," he said. "Fine."

Scarlett felt guilty for laughing at the stupid trick with the gum that the eighth graders on the bus did to Marlon. Maybe if they hadn't had such an audience, they wouldn't have gone through with it. She might cry too if she woke up to someone else's gum in her mouth.

She faced forward and handed her seatmate Patty an earbud. "Wanna listen together?" she asked. "It's the new Taylor Swift album." Scarlett had had enough of the Cheese Bus for today.

The bus pulled up to the last house on their morning route, which was just across Banditt Bridge from the school.

Paul Hacker's mom walked out to the bus with him, wearing the same Lululemon yoga pants that every mom in Flemming wore.

"I apologize," Bruno called out to her, as he opened the door.

"They're not supposed to be late," Paul's mom said, as she nudged her son onto the bus.

"Sorry, sorry, sorry," he answered in his thick Italian accent, smiling for her.

"Don't let this happen again, please," she said. "I'm on the school board, you know?"

Scarlett felt bad for Bruno. It was the first time she could remember ever being late for school because of the bus, and it was only eleven minutes after nine. They were going to be fifteen minutes late at most. The school would probably give them all late passes for first period too.

Bruno shut the door and started toward school. He revved his engine and climbed the hill on Nairn Boulevard faster than usual.

The bus came down Nairn now, also more rapidly than normal. Scarlett liked to close her eyes on the downhill and imagine she was on the Double Dragon coaster at Six Flags and then open them just as she felt the bus slide onto Banditt Drawbridge.

She felt the bus skid a bit to the left on the slick ground and from her seat right behind him, saw Bruno pull the wheel back to the right, and then to the left again to correct himself. He even veered into the other lane for a second. Just as she saw a look of concern on Bruno's face, she noticed a black car coming in the other direction.

She grabbed onto the divider between the stairs and her seat and held on as everything spun around. She barely felt any impact, but all of a sudden, she was upside down. She held on as the bus spun in mid-air, but lost her grip quickly. Scarlett had a feeling of weightlessness, then, until her whole body hit the roof of the bus. It felt like a real roller coaster now. They *were* falling.

Oh no, she thought. *Oh my God.*

CHAPTER 18

KYLE MADE THE LONG, DOWNHILL JOURNEY through the tunnel between the rung labeled *1998* and the one labeled *2016,* and then slid the silk blot into its slot. He pushed his head through and looked around eagerly. He hoped he was coming back to a world in which the people he killed were still alive . . . A world in which he would have to explain why a free man was inside a cell in Stevenson Youth Correctional in the first place.

Immediately, though, standing in his empty cell, his brain felt incredibly fuzzy. *That can't be right. Was I dreaming? Am I dreaming?* His entire memory of the bus crash felt unclear.

He saw the same picture of him with his mom at the beach on the wall over his bunk. *Shit!* If this was still his cell, it would mean his father had failed to stop the bus crash. *Wait! Stop the bus crash? Was he dreaming?* Kyle stood for a moment trying to figure out what was reality and what he might have dreamt. He also saw his list on the wall—the thirteen names from the bus.

Kyle laid down in bed, and stared at the other side of the cell. He noticed that Ochoa's training regimen was missing from the spot where it had been taped on the wall since Kyle arrived at the prison. And Ochoa's toiletries were gone. *Maybe everything was different! Maybe it hadn't been a dream.* But that would mean Ochoa was dead. And if Kyle's stuff was still there, that Sillow hadn't stopped the crash.

Kyle felt exhausted. He had no sense of what time it was, but he stretched his legs out, and extended his toes as far as he could. *The whole thing must have been a dream.*

He opened his eyes for just a second and saw his folder, with all of his newspaper clippings from the day of the accident, sitting on his foot locker. There was no doubt now that he was back in *his* cell at Stevenson Youth Correctional. Seconds later, he passed out.

Kyle opened his eyes when he felt something poking him in the belly. He saw a few sets of legs right in front of his face. All of them wore the navy blue pants of the Stevenson prison guards.

"Hey, Cash!" a voice called out, as he felt another poke in his ribs. "Get your ass up."

He was too exhausted to listen. He closed his eyes again.

Later, he was startled awake when he opened his eyes and saw four guards holding him down, while

Mrs. Wilson, the Stevenson nurse, stuck a needle into his arm. Kyle wondered why they were holding him when he had no strength to resist them. She was drawing blood from him. He looked around and realized that he was in the prison's infirmary.

When she was done drawing blood, the guards all took a step back. The five of them stood and looked at Kyle. He was still confused about what had just happened to him, but felt refreshed and awake now. His memories of the day of the crash still felt off. Not incomplete, but *too complete.* Like several memories overlapping each other.

"Hey! Sleeping beauty! Ready to wake your ass up!" a stern voice shouted. Kyle opened his eyes again. A man in a suit stepped between two officers. Kyle had never spoken to Warden Aguilar before.

The warden leaned his head down close to Kyle's face. "Where's Trevor Ochoa?"

Kyle looked the warden in the eyes. "Huh?" was all Kyle managed to get out.

"Your cellmate is missing and I need answers. You guys are friends, so tell me, where is Trevor Ochoa?"

Kyle used his whole upper body to shake his head 'no.' All of a sudden, the memory came to him so sharply he knew his trip to the past had been real. He cringed as he thought about Ochoa bringing his hands up to his ears in pain, and then, his head exploding off of his shoulders.

"No?" Warden Aguilar said indignantly. "No? What does 'no' mean?"

Kyle took a deep breath and tried to form the words. "I don't know."

"And I bet you don't know what you drank or smoked—or snorted—to make yourself completely incapacitated for the last four hours, is that right?" the warden asked. "But *we* will, as soon as this blood test comes back. And you're gonna want me to be thinking of you kindly when I have proof of whatever fucking contraband you ingested."

Kyle remembered Myrna Rachnowitz telling

him he could go back in time to stop the crash. It was all real. Nothing had been a dream.

Kyle quickly sat himself up. He needed to figure out what to tell them. He just looked at the warden, and the guards behind him and didn't say anything.

Mrs. Wilson stepped in between two of the guards. "Rapid screen is clear for drugs and alcohol," she said.

"I don't get it," the warden said, walking to the window of the room. "I don't fucking get it . . . " He turned to Kyle again. "You have *no* clue where your cellmate went? He just fucking vanished?"

After a full night of sleep, things were even clearer to Kyle. His trip through time felt a bit more like a distant memory than a recent one, but he knew for sure that it had all been real: Ochoa's head blowing up all over the pavement in Washington

Heights, Allaire tantalizing him and almost making him give up on coming back at all, and his father pressing his forearm against Kyle's throat in the white Sentra which Kyle would own many years later.

What he *couldn't* figure out was what had gone wrong. *Had Sillow just blown it off, and not shown up?* That was his best guess at the moment.

Kyle looked through his folder with all of the clippings from the accident. He knew all of them word for word. All of the obituaries. Even the names of the surviving loved ones. *Lucilla Pasquale . . . Jennifer Hacker . . . Alberto Costello . . .*

He read through the front page article from the *Times-Gazette* from the day after the crash looking for something. Some clue as to what had gone wrong. He knew the first paragraph of the article almost by heart:

Flemming, NY (AP)—A traffic accident occurred yesterday morning when an automobile collided with a school bus in Flemming, NY, killing fourteen people in total. The bus flipped over the barricade of a bridge above Banditt River and fell forty feet into the water. The only survivor of the crash, which occurred shortly after nine o'clock, was the driver of the Black Audi A4 which struck the bus. Authorities have declined to comment as to whether the driver may have been impaired at the time of the accident.

It was on his third reading of the article in a row that Kyle noticed it. He needed to consider every word, looking for any slight change. *There had to be at least one thing that changed as a result of the trip through time*, Kyle thought to himself . . . And, that's what it turned out to be. One thing: a single word.

*The only survivor of the crash which occurred just **after** nine o'clock.*

There it was! The original accident took place at 8:59. Kyle knew it because he'd gotten to see the autopsy reports for each student during his trial. His lawyer had resisted showing them to Kyle at first, but he was obliged to do what his client asked. Eight of the thirteen people on the bus had been given a time of death of 8:59 AM, just as the collision happened. Five others had been found to survive the initial crash, only to drown in Banditt River below.

Quickly, though, Kyle's excitement faded. *So what?* he thought, the more he considered it. So, it had been a few minutes later, but the accident had still happened. The clippings and the obituaries were all still there. Everyone was still dead. He'd been given the chance to change everything and he'd failed.

He spent the rest of Sunday afternoon in his bunk. Word would spread soon enough that Ochoa had escaped and Kyle wondered how he was going to protect himself against Stevenson's many gangs without Ochoa having his back.

He heard the lock on his cell door turning and wished Ochoa would walk through.

Officer Radbourn walked in instead. "Cash Man, what the hell happened? Warden's saying you got high and helped Ochoa escape. What the fuck?"

Kyle wished he could just tell Radbourn everything. He wanted to tell *someone* everything.

"None of it's true," Kyle said. "My tox screening came back clean. And, I have no clue about Ochoa. I'm just as surprised as you are."

"Whatever," Radbourn said. "Anyway, you've got a visitor."

Kyle sat up. "Who?" he asked.

CHAPTER 19

FEBRUARY 4, 2016

moments later

A FEW DAYS AGO, WHEN SILLOW VISITED, KYLE looked through him at first. He was no more familiar than a stranger.

Now, even with the receding hairline and a face that had every minute of the last eighteen years stamped across it, Kyle knew him immediately.

"Hey," Sillow said as Kyle sat down.

He waited for Radbourn to back out of earshot, and then Kyle leaned his head in close. "I went back, didn't I? Tell me I'm not crazy."

Sillow nodded. "I came here yesterday. I tried to tell you not to. Whole thing was doomed from the start."

"What do you mean, doomed?" Kyle asked.

"As that day got closer," Sillow said. "Every little thing that could go wrong, did. My flight was delayed. Then, the landing gear got stuck and we had to land without it. After I gave a statement to police at the airport about the crash, the cab I took to my hotel broke down. And, that lady . . . "

Kyle shifted in his seat. Everything had been real. There was no doubt that Ochoa was really dead. "What lady?"

"This lady showed up at your house that morning—"

"Blond? Black baseball cap?" Kyle asked.

"Yeah," Sillow said. "I locked you in the bathroom, like you told me to. You and your friend didn't even try to break out of there. I think you were too high—smelled like a fuckin' reggae concert in that hallway."

"So, what happened?" Kyle asked.

"The woman broke into the house right after I locked you guys in and stuck a knife in my face.

She went up and unlocked the door. Forced me into the trunk of your car for a few hours so I couldn't do anything. Then, she put me in a taxi back to the airport and threatened to kill me if she saw me again. By the time I got down to JFK a few hours later, the bus crash was all over the news."

When he thought back to the morning of the crash now, Kyle vaguely remembered being locked in the bathroom. It was fuzzy though, like his memories from traveling back in time. He remembered the woman's voice talking to him through the door and asking him to count to 200.

"I'm sorry, Kyle. I'm sorry I let you down again," Sillow said.

"Who is she?" Kyle asked. "Why would she want the accident to happen?"

"She told me it had to," Sillow said.

"Dammit!" Kyle said, pounding the table.

"Hey!" a guard called over. "Knock it off!"

Why wouldn't Myrna have warned him if there was going to be someone there trying to stand in the way of their plan? Kyle closed his eyes and tried to think clearly about his time in 1998. He remembered seeing the blond woman watching from a distance when Ochoa died, and then again in the parking garage of the hospital where Sillow worked, sprinting toward him, and then turning and running away just as quickly.

"I went up to New York so I could get past my guilt for being such a shitty father," Sillow said. "But eventually, I started to get jealous that you got to go back and try to fix what you've done wrong," Sillow continued. "I started to wish I got that chance."

"We blew it though," Kyle said, exasperated. "We had the chance to change everything, and all we managed to do was delay the crash about fifteen minutes."

"We did somethin' then, son," Sillow said. "We changed somethin' . . . " Kyle was surprised that Sillow looked excited. *What did it matter?* And, he wasn't sure how he felt about Sillow suddenly calling him 'son.'

Sillow put his hand on Kyle's forearm. "Listen, I know how much I messed up when you were little. I didn't know either of my parents. I was lucky I had an aunt who gave a shit, but instead of correcting my parents' mistakes, I just did the same old shit."

"Sillow . . . Dad . . . whatever . . . I don't care about that right now," Kyle said. "Everyone's still dead."

"But, you tried! And, I tried," Sillow said. "We even gave those kids a few extra minutes . . . And now, I'm trying now to make things right with you."

Kyle put his head in his hands. It was too much for him right now. He'd prayed for years that his father would come back like this. Anytime there was an unexpected knock on the door growing up, he hoped. Every time he got an interesting looking piece of mail. Every single time the phone rang . . .

He looked up at Sillow and saw tears in his eyes.

"What's wrong?" Kyle asked.

"Don't you understand? I've been waiting to have this conversation with you for two years," Sillow said. "Waiting to have *any* conversation with you."

Kyle thought about how they'd each messed up. He got to go back in time to try to erase his one, huge mistake. Sillow didn't have that option, so here he was. How could he blame his father for wanting a second chance too?

"We're good," Kyle said. "I told you we were square if you did what I asked."

"But, it didn't work," Sillow said. "And, I don't wanna be square with you. I wanna be your father. That's why it kills me that I couldn't get this done for you."

"You showed up, dad," Kyle said.

"Showed up?" Sillow asked. "That woman didn't weigh a hundred pounds wet and I let her stop me."

"You did all you could," Kyle answered.

"Maybe there's another way," Sillow said. "A way we could get one more chance."

"Myrna, the woman who sent me back, said this was it," Kyle answered. "I'm lucky I got a second chance. Most people only get one."

Sillow looked at Kyle and smiled. "People say a lot of things, son . . . Thing to remember is, they ain't always true."

TO BE CONTINUED . . .